GW00858347

The
QUEST for the
CRYSTAL SKULLS

Lynn Florkiewicz

Pen Press

First published in Great Britain by Pen Press

ISBN13: 978-1-906710-09-5

Printed and bound in UK by Cpod, Trowbridge, Wiltshire
Pen Press is an imprint of Indepenpress Publishing Limited
25 Eastern Place
Brighton
BN2 1GJ

A catalogue record of this book is available from
the British Library

Cover design by Jacqueline Abromeit

DEDICATIONS AND

ACKNOWLEDGEMENTS

Writing this book has been an exciting journey. However, it would have remained unfinished without the encouragement of family and friends. A huge thank you to:

My husband, Tad, who re-ignited my passion for writing. I couldn't begin to explain how much your love and support has helped me.

Mum and Dad who have quietly encouraged my creativity.

Friends and family who show so much interest in my writing; Malcolm and Marion, Joy and Rod, Carolyn and Stewart, Rod, Mary-Linda, Steve and Anne, Betty Cocard.

Bookworm Ashna Hurynag who, between school projects and homework, tirelessly read through the final draft.

Brian Winston for your on-going help.

Stewart Harvey, for setting up my website.

The helpful and approachable team at penpress.

And finally, Native Americans - for your historical culture and spirituality. It is the wisdom and passion of your ancestors that inspired me to write The Quest for the Crystal Skulls. I've enjoyed brief moments with many tribal people and hope I've done your beliefs justice in this story.

ABOUT THE AUTHOR

Lynn lives and works in West Sussex. Her interest in writing began initially through the folk music scene of the 70s and 80s, where she performed her own songs and guitar instrumentals around the folk clubs.

After numerous appearances across Southern England, Lynn answered an ad in the Melody Maker and found herself being one of only two women based in the UK to be featured on an album called 'Women's Guitar Workshop'. A solo album followed, along with a tour of New England, New York, Washington and California, singing in coffee houses, clubs and universities. Back in the UK, further guest appearances took place at festivals and on local and BBC radio.

After getting married, Lynn put the touring and song writing bug behind her and turned her hand to writing stories. A number of her short stories and articles have been published in various magazines but her passion is pure and simple - adventure stories for children. Coupling this with her interest in Native America and the unexplained, prompted the idea for this novel.

She's available for talks, interviews and, if you ask nicely, the odd song!

If you'd like to find out more, visit her website at:

www.lynnflorkiewicz.co.uk.

CHAPTER ONE

Something glinted in the sand ahead. Fourteen-year-old Tom Carver dropped his chocolate wrapper and jumped onto the beach.

The previous night's treacherous sea had calmed. He smiled; there was always something churned up in the squall and this looked more interesting than the usual cola tins.

Quickening his pace along the Cornish shoreline, driftwood in one hand, rucksack in the other, he focussed on the object ahead and pondered his day. This is better than school. Hope Jack's covered for me. He recalled his best friend's parting words:

"Just once more, Tom. They get right suspicious when you bunk off the same lessons. You can't just pitch up for what you want."

"Well, what good's drama and art? Load o' rubbish."

"It'll all be rubbish if you're suspended."

Tom had shrugged. "Who cares? It's all boring."

A small wave splashed across his feet. *"Clanni sha,"* it whispered. He stopped, listened and shrugged.

Closer now. He squinted at the glass as an unnatural brightness created prisms of colour in the sunlight. The sea always gave up glimpses of people's lives; but this looked different. Dropping everything, he knelt and gouged the sand from around the object.

"Come on," he muttered. The sea trickled across his ankles and sucked the glass down.

"Oh no you don't." He rammed his hands into the sand. Tiny granules clogged his fingernails as he pushed deeper and

1

traced along strange ridges and hollows. Must be some sort of carving. At the base he linked his fingers. Got you now.

"Ow." He winced as his hands clamped to the glass. Dazzling lights flared as a strange landscape flashed before him. Searing pains shot through his head with such force he had to squeeze his eyes shut to stop from crying out. The pain vanished.

Opening his eyes, he found himself on top of a high ridge. The earth trembled violently. He threw himself to the ground and stared wildly at his strange surroundings.

"Mum!"

Cracks appeared in the earth alongside and he scrambled away, watching, searching, hoping for something familiar.

"Dad? Dad!"

His stomach clenched as the ground split open. He clambered clumsily as stones and loose earth fell into the newly formed abyss. Swallowing a wave of nausea, he went to run but tripped and crashed to the ground, flinching as his head hit the dirt.

Wiping blood from his forehead, he looked down at his bruised and grazed knuckles. His pulse roared in his ears, his senses desperate for something familiar.

A young voice shouted feebly, "Help."

Tom spun round. A young girl in a torn, summer dress stumbled towards him, her brown hair matted with dust and rubble. He held a hand out.

"Don't worry. Here, take my hand."

The searing pain jolted him again. He squeezed his eyes shut. It disappeared.

Peering out, his tense shoulders relaxed as he found himself back on the beach. Slumping wearily, questions shot at him like popcorn in a microwave. What the hell was that? What happened? He clenched the wet sand – clinging to reality – muttering.

"It's a dream, just a dream." He swallowed anxiously.

The cool water sent chills through him. He studied his hands – no bruising, no grazes and, feeling his head, no cut. He checked his watch. Only seconds had passed.

It glinted more brightly now.

"Clannah khall clanni sha."

He frowned suspiciously at the glass and touched it warily with the tip of his finger. Phew! Nothing. Grabbing the piece of driftwood, he rammed it into the sand and began levering.

As the glass surfaced Tom wondered what it could be. If it's valuable, I'll sell it and get away from this tin pot town. Lost in a daydream, he squatted on the sands plotting his escape. Finally, he looked at the object and, with a gasp, dropped it.

Scrambling to his feet, he stared open-mouthed at a perfectly formed skull. The empty eye sockets stared back as the breaking waves whispered.

"Clannah khall clanni sha."

Tom flinched. The waves sucked the skull down. He stooped to retrieve it, cradling it as he stepped on to drier sand. He held the heavy skull awkwardly.

"Clannah khall clanni sha."

Tom let it go. It fell to the sand and stared silently, but Tom knew.

The whispering had come from inside.

A piercing shriek resounded across the beach and Tom spun to see a crazy hermit, with torn, brown robes, running toward him. His thin, bony arms flailed and his wild hair and long, unruly beard resembled a mass of grey candyfloss.

When he reached Tom, he hopped as if dancing on hot coals, chanting hysterically.

"The crystal skull, the crystal skull, the chosen one, the chosen one, it has begun, the chosen one."

With a long, dirty index finger, he bent down and drew a huge circle in the sand. Taking out a wooden flute, he played

3

an oddly mesmerising tune, then bounded around the circle repeating his rhyme.

"The crystal skull, the crystal skull, the chosen one, the chosen one, it has begun, the chosen one."

"Clannah khall clanni sha."

"Psh, psh. Pick it up! Pick it up! It speaks, it speaks. Quickly. Quickly. Psh, psh."

Tom scooped up the skull but kept his eyes firmly on the strange, sinewy man who beckoned him.

"Come. Come."

The man raced toward the dunes at the back of the beach. Tom frowned. Who's he to tell me what to do? He's a complete nutcase. Pulling his shoulders back, he shouted across to him.

"You're not having it you know, it's mine. I found it."

The crazy man turned.

"Oh God," Tom mumbled as his stomach flipped. He hugged the skull closer, staring at the hermit's every move, unsure of what to do as the man's manic form came closer.

Tom grabbed his rucksack and got ready to sprint. The man stopped within inches of him and thrust his head forward. Tom stepped back and held his breath; not only was this man loony, but he stunk as well.

The old man tilted his head and smirked.

"It doesn't belong to you," he announced smarmily. "It belongs to the ancients, they wanted you to find it."

Tom sneered. "The ancients? What're you talking about? You're off your 'ead."

The old man turned on his heels, pulled out his flute and danced away like the Pied Piper. The tune forced its way into Tom's head, encouraging him to follow.

He looked at the empty beach, then gazed into the skull's sunken sockets. What are you then? Ancients, chosen one, what's he on about? The man stopped playing the flute but the tune carried on the breeze. The melody pranced around his head, urging him to follow.

Tom contemplated. He knew the answer to his questions would only be found with this strange, gangly man.

"Clannah khall clanni sha,"

"COVER IT, COVER IT," the old man screamed.

Tom ripped off his T-shirt and covered the skull.

"QUICKLY, QUICKLY."

Tom rolled his eyes as he trudged through the sand.

"Oh, wind your neck in," he replied, "you don't 'ave to throw a wobbler."

"Psh, psh."

Tom shook his head. "Tom Carver, what're you gettin' yourself into?"

CHAPTER TWO

Tom approached the old man's den cautiously. When he bunked off school he always came to the beach but he'd never noticed this before. On first glance he realised he wouldn't; it was so well camouflaged. Hidden among the dunes at the back of the beach and shielded by overgrown pampas grass, the entrance appeared invisible. It was only by following the indented footsteps of the old man that he found it.

Peering through the entrance, his eyes adjusted to the dimmed light. He stepped inside, stooping to avoid thick chunks of driftwood that supported the arched opening.

"Wow," he reeled, marvelling at the ingenuity of the man and a little envious that this wonderful cave wasn't his own.

The hermit twitched and jumped but Tom focussed on the den – dug deep into the dunes. Sand-ingrained threadbare carpets overlapped on the floor creating pale, discoloured, patterns. Discarded wooden planks from broken boats lined the walls haphazardly. He sidestepped the small buoys and lanterns that hung precariously from old fishing nets stretched across the ceiling. It smelt salty and damp, like an ancient trawler.

His eyes narrowed at objects perched on uneven shelves. They looked incredibly old: vases, bottles, sculptures, swords, pistols, and…a shrunken head! Catching his breath, he stared at the old man, who chuckled. Tom scowled.

"What? What's so funny?"

The hermit bounded from the cave and Tom went to follow but froze when a voice spoke from behind.

"You amuse him," came a man's posh, chirpy reply.

Tom swung round. "Who're you, and who's that nutter?"

The man stepped out from the shadows. Tom studied him closely. He looked like an intrepid explorer from Victorian times: tall, slim and upright, with a huge handlebar moustache curled up at the ends. On his head he wore a tattered Panama hat. His light Chinos had their hems rolled up from his bare feet and he folded the sleeves back on his shirt. Tom stepped back as the man came closer. He spoke clearly and effortlessly.

"My name is Davenport. Brigadier Charles Clive Bartholomew Davenport. Davvers to my friends, and that includes you, Tom Carver."

"How d'you know my name?"

"I find it helps to know who's who when you live on the beach and, as you spend about as much time here as I do, I make it my business to know."

Tom smirked. No one spoke like that anymore, surely. He sounds like one of those old BBC announcers, talking posh without moving his lips. He peered outside – where did that mad bloke go? Davvers followed his gaze.

"I think his name's Zannor. Odd that, haven't seen the fellow in years then he pitched up out of nowhere a couple of days ago."

"I've never seen him before. Mad is he?"

"Well, he's not from around here."

Tom eyed him suspiciously – this was all very strange. Davvers smiled. A wide, beaming smile emphasised by the curling moustache, and the whitest of teeth. The smile reached his sparkling hazel eyes.

"Don't worry, Tom, I'm not crazy – it suits my lifestyle to have people think it though."

Tom nodded thoughtfully. He seemed okay. Davvers pointed to a tattered wing-backed chair and grabbed a matching one from the back of the cave. He sat down and gestured to Tom.

"Please. I don't get many visitors."

Tom ignored the seat, drawn instead to the items in the cave. They were labelled, like in a museum. Davvers lit a small camping gas stove and put a kettle of water on to boil.

"Tea?"

"Have you got something fizzy?"

Davvers glanced up apologetically. Tom shrugged.

"Tea's fine."

He wandered across to the objects. The labels, written with an old-fashioned fountain pen, had faded, but the objects held a fascination. A small Aztec rug, brightly coloured in yellows, reds and turquoise, had been weaved with geometric designs and flat-topped pyramids; cottonwood Kachina dolls carved by the Hopi tribe in Arizona, neatly decorated with feathers and hoops and dressed as clowns, birds and buffalo; smooth black Inca vases from Peru; figures in red and ochre gowns, capes and feather headdresses. He grimaced at a dead cobra pickled in an elongated jar.

Davvers shouted across, "Killed that blighter in the jungle. Little tyke was just about to bite."

Tom moved along slowly. Mayan drawings from Central America, faded portraits of Egyptian kings, aboriginal sculptures from the deserts of Australia.

He picked up an old black and white photograph showing a young army officer sporting a handlebar moustache and a pristine Panama hat standing in front of the pyramids. Several National Geographic covers showed the same young man. Davvers sat up proudly.

"I was in the army for thirty years. Retired now. Fortunate enough to travel the world and lead many an expedition. It's those experiences that led me to the path I'm on now."

Tom sniggered. "What, living rough?"

"Don't judge me on appearance, Tom."

Tom shrugged. Look like you're living rough to me.

Keeping the skull wrapped, he sat down, observing the man prepare tea. His eyes held a charm among the weathered wrinkles of age and wisdom. He handed Tom a delicate bone china cup.

"Tell me, Tom. You're on the beach most days."

"So?"

"How old are you?"

"Fourteen."

"Friends?"

Tom grimaced. "School."

"And that's where you should be, yes?"

Tom shrugged, wishing Davvers would change the subject.

"I know why you don't like school, of course," Davvers continued, "you think it's boring; you're not taught what you want to know; you're much happier outside, intolerant of teachers and anyone–"

"All right, don't go on about it. It's nothing to do with you why I don't go."

Davvers held up his hands. "At ease, Tom. I'm not judging you. My guess is that you've an ambition that school doesn't provide, yes?"

Tom shrugged again.

"It's all right, old chap, I'm not about to turn you in. It's rare to find someone your age outside so much."

Tom looked at the floor. "I like being outside. I'm supposed to be in art and drama but it's right boring, same as everything in this place."

Tom glowered as Davvers laughed and reached across for a clay pipe.

"I see a mirror image of myself in you, Tom." He carefully prepared the pipe, took a few puffs and contemplated. "Art and drama will, undoubtedly, do little to spark your particular interests."

9

Tom shrugged, but was quietly pleased that Davvers agreed.

"You play truant because you discover more out here." He leaned forward. "The seas are more luring than a textbook; the air is fresher than a classroom; the land has more life than a playground." His eyes sparkled. "You've no right being bored, Tom."

"I'll be bored if I want."

"Why?"

"Everything's boring. Teachers think I'm a waster. Mum and Dad are always working. No one bothers about me." He looked at Davvers. "I prefer being outside. I do my bit. I earn wages on Jenner's farm, collecting eggs, feeding chickens."

"Better than drawing lifeless fruit in a dusty art class, eh?"

Tom chewed his lip. Why did Davvers understand and his parents didn't? Davvers pointed at Tom's lap.

"What is it that you're so keen to keep secret?"

Tom drew the skull closer and scrutinised Davvers. He might know if it's worth something. Might even know what it is. He put his cup down, tugged the T-shirt and revealed the skull. Davvers' pipe fell from his mouth.

"Good lord!" he exclaimed as he sat forward and carefully cradled the skull in his hands. "Where did you get this?"

"I found it. It's mine, you're not 'aving it."

Davvers returned the skull, rushed to the back of the cave and rummaged around the bric-a-brac and blankets. Tom stared after him.

"What're you doin'?"

"Ha!" Davvers pulled at something. "Tell me, when you found it, is that when you saw Zannor?"

"Yeah, but he didn't say it was his. I found it. Is it worth somethin'?"

Davvers bounded back. Tom turned his nose up at the moth-eaten bundle he'd returned with.

"Leaping up and down, was he?"

"Yeah, right mental, calling me the chosen one – talking about ancients."

Davvers' face drained of colour. "Good lord!"

"What? Do you know what it is?"

"I've heard things, legends, when I was in Central America, in the jungle. I didn't think they were true."

A pain stabbed through Tom's ears. He squeezed his eyes shut as a black fog swirled and clung to him like glue. Soot filtered down his nose and throat and he coughed and retched violently.

"Clannah khall clanni sha, gather us in, the thirteen, the thirteen, gather us in."

The pain vanished.

"Tom? You all right, old chap?"

Tom gripped the chair. "Did I just disappear?"

"What?"

"Did you hear voices?"

Tom could see that Davvers thought he was completely mad. He'd obviously not been anywhere. What the hell's going on? He massaged his forehead. This is insane!

"Tom? You sure you're all right?"

Davvers put a hand on his shoulder but Tom immediately pushed it away and sat up straight, forcing the fear from his mind.

"Look I'm all right, prob'ly a migraine or something. Anyway, you were saying somethin' about legends."

"Yes, I thought the legends were just stories. I was in Belize." He began unfolding the bundle. "The legends speak of a chosen one."

As Davvers lifted the last fold, Tom gasped. There, among the dusty pleats, sat a second skull. Tom gazed at it.

"What do you think, Tom?"

Tom studied the skull on his lap. Cool to the touch, his hands slid across the smoothest of surfaces and felt their way around the carving. The jawbone moved but didn't appear detachable, the eye sockets were perfectly formed. He saw no cracks, blemishes or chips, only natural markings and air bubbles.

"Well. It's glass. Surprised it's not broken. Thought this jaw bone would've come away."

"It's not glass, Tom. I know very little but I can tell you that these are made from one solid piece of crystal. The most difficult material to carve without shattering."

Tom turned it over in his hands looking for faults, but he couldn't see any.

"So what's the legend?"

"Ancient civilisations speak of a chosen one."

"Well, what's that mean?"

"I didn't believe any of it. Tribal superstition."

"So what is it?" Tom pulled a face. "We're all cursed?"

Davvers sat back and puffed on his pipe. Through wispy smoke, his smiling eyes became deadly serious.

"The chosen one is a descendant of those that made the skulls. They're sought to help stop mankind from destroying the planet."

CHAPTER THREE

Tom clenched his teeth and frantically covered the skull.

"You're just as crazy as that idiot out there. Load of rubbish. I'm not some stupid kid, you know, I do know when someone's winding me up."

"Then go. It wasn't me who invited you here."

Tom grabbed his stuff and got up, but he couldn't leave. Random thoughts circled like sheep gathered around a pen. They're there but none want to take the plunge and go in. Davvers handed him more tea.

"Do you know what crystal is, Tom?" he asked chirpily.

Tom shook his head in a daze.

"It's a natural rock. You've heard of quartz watches?" Tom nodded. "Well, that's quartz crystal. They use it in electronics – clocks, computers, space satellites, that sort of thing."

Tom sat back down and unwrapped the skull.

"What you're holding there could be as old as time itself."

Tom traced the skull's outline. "What else d'you know?"

"Only that they were made by ancient civilisations. Native Americans, the Incas, Mayans–"

"Mayans?"

"Yes, from Central America. It's great stuff, human sacrifices, chopping people's heads off, giving their hearts to the gods."

"Bloody hell! Do they still do that?"

"No, they're extinct now. The Incas lived in Peru, you know, where Paddington Bear comes from."

"I'm fourteen, not four."

Davvers smiled apologetically. "The Native Americans, of course, are alive and well and kicking about all over North America. The Hopi tribe have some skulls. I keep meaning to send this across to Ed, a Hopi friend of mine. It should be with them really." Davvers relit his pipe. "The legend says that the skulls communicate."

Tom almost dropped his cup.

"How?"

"Let me pose a question to you, Tom. If you lived four hundred years ago and found a DVD, one of those discs, what would you think it was? Remember, this is a time when electricity didn't exist."

Tom contemplated. "Some sort of mat or decoration or somethin'."

"Exactly. No one back then would know what it was and even if they thought it held something, they wouldn't know how to get it."

"Because they didn't have the technology?"

"Bang on, Tom."

"But we've got electricity."

"Crystals are capable of electric impulse, of storing information. They didn't need to use electricity like we do."

"When you found that one, did it talk to you?"

Davvers laughed. "Good lord, no." His smile disappeared. "Why, did yours?"

Tom shrunk back and shook his head.

"I tell you one thing though. Zannor came racing through the jungle like some wild ape. He's a link. Must be. Pity he can't string a sentence together."

"Does the number thirteen mean anything to you?"

"No. Should it?"

Tom shook his head as Davvers placed the skulls on the

floor. Within seconds, a faint blue glow shimmered in them. Tom pushed his chair back, his heart thumping.

"No, it's some sort of trick. Whoever made these, well they couldn't, could they? They were primitive – savages. They didn't know anythin'."

"How could savages carve such perfect images?"

Tom snarled. "You've got all the answers."

"I haven't though, Tom. You should know more than me if Zannor's calling you the chosen one. If that's right, then you're a descendant."

Tom looked at him. Descendant? It's drivel; he's just some delusional tramp. But that didn't explain the visions, the ranting hermit, the whispering voice. The skulls shimmered in the dim light. He closed his eyes and sighed.

He came in here looking for answers and all he'd got so far were more questions.

CHAPTER FOUR

"So," said Mr Griffith, in a bellowing Welsh accent, "decided to grace us with your presence have you?"

Tom's head teacher struggled to keep up with him. The veins on his shiny, bald head throbbed as his blood pressure rocketed.

"Three times you've been absent this week, giving us all manner of excuses, and what're you doing? Skiving, that's what. Because you can't be bothered."

Tom turned a corner and snuck into the cleaner's cupboard. He heard Griffith shout down the empty corridor.

"You're a waster. I'm not having it. D'you hear?" He plodded back, mumbling. "I'll throw the book at you, boy, you see if I don't."

Tom sneaked out at lesson change.

"Bonkers," he said to Jack as they waited for their teacher.

"Heart attack waiting to happen," said Jack. "I've heard he's on mental pills – having a breakdown. Anyway, what're you doing here, you don't do French."

"Somethin's happened."

"D'you want a crisp?"

Tom rolled his eyes. Jack was the same lean build as him but always stuffing his face.

"Stop eating, this is serious."

"You're not being expelled are you? I do my best to cover, but you keep skipping the same lessons."

"It's nothin' to do with school. D'you know anything about crystals?"

Jack let out a laugh. "You're not going all new age are you?"

"This isn't funny, Jack!"

"All right, keep your hair on."

Tom told Jack about the skull but decided to stay quiet about the visions for fear of ridicule. Jack munched his crisps and listened carefully. At the end, he had one question.

"So, d'you think this Davvers bloke is off his head?"

"I know, sounds weird don't it?"

"Weird? It sounds pretty far-fetched. Ancient computers, the chosen one, saving the planet. He belongs in a comic."

Tom looked away and ran his hands through his hair. Jack didn't believe him. Why should he? It sounded complete rubbish. The visions would convince him. But if he thought Davvers was mad, he'd think he was too. He opened his text book.

"Maybe you're right."

Jack tapped on the computer as Tom slumped back in his chair.

"Christ, you're such a swot. I thought you'd be a bit interested?"

Jack smiled. "If you're not sure about something, go on the Internet." He twisted the screen round.

"Bloody hell!" Tom stared at page after page of websites about crystal skulls. Jack clicked into one, scanning the text.

"Quartz crystal skulls, discovered in many ancient places, hold the knowledge of the universe."

Tom leaned forward. "What's that say?"

"The skulls are piezo-electric, used in modern day technology. What's piezo-electric?"

Tom shook his head. "Dunno. But Davvers said something about storing information."

Tom pointed further down. "Try that."

A sharp pain skewered into Tom. He squeezed his eyes shut as the now familiar spasms dropped him into another vision. He opened his eyes in horror. A tornado, wider than a football pitch, churned methodically, spitting remnants of a small town through the air like confetti.

"Clannah khall clanni sha. Gather me in, the thirteen, the halls of antiquity, halls of antiquity, take me, take me—"

Tom covered his ears and dropped to the floor.

"Stop! Please."

Invisible hands shook him and distant voices shouted.

"TOM!"

Tom opened his eyes and saw Jack kneeling beside him.

After an hour in the medical centre, Tom began feeling better. The visions had sapped his energy but not his thoughts, which ran through him like ticker-tape. Halls of antiquity? Gather me in. Gather what in? As he rested his head back, Jack raced in and glared at him.

"What happened back there?"

Tom shrugged, trying to stay blasé. "Dunno, bad headache."

Jack shook his head. "No. That was no headache." He drew up a chair, took out a scrappy piece of paper from his pocket and began reading.

"The Fourth World, come together, Mother Earth, the end of the Fourth World, save Mother Earth." He looked at Tom. "Say that a lot when you've got headaches?"

Tom stared at Jack. "What else 'ave you written? My friend's gone mad?"

Jack leaned forward. "I typed 'Fourth World' into Google. Did this Davvers bloke mention the Mayans or the Hopi?"

Tom sat up as Jack continued.

"These worlds are Mayan prophecies. The first was destroyed by volcanoes and fires, the second by drought,

18

the third by floods." Jack looked at him. "The fourth will be destroyed by the actions of mankind."

"And we're in the fourth."

Jack nodded. "Tom, that was no headache. You need to tell me everything."

* * *

That night Tom dreamed. He sat cross-legged under an ancient sycamore tree. An elderly Native American man sat opposite and spoke to him in a rasping voice.

"Young warrior, gather courage and bring the skulls together. You are a descendant. They must unite. Only the chosen one can take those to be found. Transcend your doubts. Listen to those who impart their wisdom. Be brave in your quest."

Tom sat up with a start. Beads of sweat ran down his back and the skull pulsated a soft blue light around the room.

CHAPTER FIVE

Saturday morning, Tom wheeled his bike out and glared at the empty house. Why did Mum and Dad work so much? We're not that hard up, surely. He slammed the gate shut.

At the promenade, Jack waited by an ice-cream van munching on a cornet. A few dogs chased the tide and ran playfully along the wide expanse of sand.

"So where's this Davvers bloke?" Jack said.

They chained their bikes to the railings then jumped onto the light powdery sand. Tom studied the tall grasses of the dunes, but couldn't see any sort of cave. It couldn't have disappeared. He looked across at Jack.

"I can't see the opening."

"You sure it's this bit and not further on?"

Tom nodded and pointed to where he'd entered before. He frowned, took a few steps back and scratched his head. Suddenly, the tall grasses rustled and Davvers, complete with Panama hat, stepped out.

"Morning, Tom." He beckoned them in with some urgency and the two boys jogged over. "Good bit of camouflage, what? Only open up when no one's about. Come in and take a pew."

Tom grinned as Jack gazed around the cave in amazement. It was good to have him here. Although he'd questioned the visions, Tom hoped to put that right today. Davvers held out two bottles.

"Something fizzy," he said as he gestured for them to sit down.

Tom sat on the frayed bits of carpet and tugged at Jack, who finally joined him as Davvers made himself tea.

"So, Tom, introductions I think."

"This is my best mate, Jack Newton. I told him about the skulls. Jack, this is Brigadier Davenport, but you can call him Davvers."

Davvers shook Jack's hand warmly. "Welcome, Jack Newton. A sturdy name and a sturdy handshake. Would you prefer tea?"

Jack shook his head.

"The British Army's most celebrated refreshment – when on duty that is." He winked at them.

Tom and Jack smirked at each other. Davvers settled back in his chair and lit his pipe. "So, Tom. You came back."

"Yes, sir." He didn't know why he said 'sir' but it sounded right. For some reason he respected Davvers and calling him 'sir' seemed natural. Davvers puffed on his pipe.

"Tom, I can't help you with any of this. You know as much as I do."

"Well actually, we found out a bit more."

Tom told Davvers what they'd discovered. Through it all, Davvers nodded and smiled with quiet enthusiasm. At the end, Jack leaned forward.

"D'you know what piezo-electric is?"

"Well, I'm not scientific myself but I think it means that the crystal is capable of producing electric."

"You mentioned Native Americans before," Tom said.

Davvers' eyes lit up. "Ah, yes, fantastic people, very into nature, Mother Earth…"

Tom tensed. "Mother Earth!"

"Yes, Mother Earth. They're very into the environment; they consider the earth, and the animals that share it, extremely sacred. Equal to man, so to speak."

Tom undid his rucksack and took the skull out. "Can we put the skulls together again?"

Davvers retrieved his skull and placed it on the floor next to Tom's. The skulls shimmered; a faint blue hue flowed between them.

"Wow," Jack mumbled.

"I want to try something." Tom hesitated. "Davvers, d'you mind leaving me and Jack on our own?"

Davvers leapt up. "Right-ho. I'll just be outside; yell if you need anything." He picked up his tea and went. Jack look at Tom.

"What're you gonna do?"

"I'm gonna try and communicate with 'em. Then you'll know what I'm talking about."

"Communicate!"

Tom nodded and swallowed anxiously. Getting comfortable, his hands hovered above the skulls. He got Jack to do the same.

"Clannah khall clanni sha," Tom whispered gently.

He repeated it again and again. With every chant the blue hue darkened and spread further into the crystal, the deepening aqua enhancing its intricate fine lines.

Tom lowered their hands onto the crystal.

Touching the surface, he found himself under water. He gasped but the water flowed by with no threat. Crossing his eyes, he tried to watch himself breathe. A shoal of sea bass swam by and he looked around in confusion. This must be an ocean, but there're structures here. Through the murky water, ghostly Victorian buildings stood alongside modern office blocks. The hollow windows stared bleakly. He imagined stingrays and sharks lurking there ready to pounce.

Rusty red double-decker busses and black cabs stood empty, seaweed clinging to their mirrors and bumpers. Tom's mind raced. It looks like London, but that's impossible.

With some effort he waded through the water. Molluscs and crabs clung to the walls. Eels slithered by, oblivious to his curiosity. Brick walls and motor cars were being transformed into brightly coloured coral. Kelp forests grew where trees once stood.

Ahead, he saw three tall brick arches where cars would have driven through. Words had been carved in the brickwork but time had taken their meaning. Swimming through the arches, he came across a huge square surrounded by ornate buildings. A church, with its spire pointing heavenward, opened its doors for worshippers that would never arrive. In the middle of the square a tall column rose up toward the surface.

Tom gawped. Nelson's column! It is London.

He gazed up at the crumbling statue. The huge bronze lions that protected the admiral were now odd shaped mounds of moss and seaweed. He cleared the growth away to allow one proud beast to look across its domain for the first time in years. Tom looked around desperately. Why's it under water?

He pushed off and swam to the surface. The tip of the Millennium wheel peeked out of the ocean. Whatever had happened had devastated the city.

A wave of tiredness swept over him and, closing his eyes, he drifted into the depths, losing consciousness along the way. Seconds later, he saw the fishing net ceiling and Jack staring at him.

"You all right, mate?"

Tom could barely open his eyes.

"I feel like I've been drugged."

Jack handed him a drink and some crisps. "Get some food inside you."

Tom rested his head back and swigged some cola.

"You look as if you went off into some sort of trance," Jack said.

Tom grabbed his arm. "D'you me… Weren't you there? Didn't you see anything?"

Jack shook his head. "No, mate, nothing. What'd you see?"

"I saw London underwater, the whole city had drowned."

Tom closed his eyes in frustration. Jack got up and called Davvers in.

"Davvers, d'you know what all these visions are about?"

"What visions?"

Tom glared at Jack. "It's nothing."

Jack returned the glare.

"Nothing? Davvers, he's had visions, heard voices, all sorts of things. What's happening to him?"

Davvers frowned and sat down. He opened a large, round tin and offered them cake.

"I think better when I eat. D'you want some?"

"Yes please," Jack said enthusiastically, delving in for a piece. Tom shook his head.

"A rather lovely lady who lives up on the hill baked it."

Tom felt sick. Is this the first sign of madness? Why didn't Jack see it? Why is this happening? Davvers stroked his moustache as he looked at Tom.

"I don't know what your visions are, Tom. And the voices? Well, I've told you what I know. The legends tell of a chosen one. Perhaps this is proof."

Tom sat back, contemplating. Remembering the voices and the message they'd given, he nodded slowly.

"I've to bring the skulls together. They keep saying 'gather me in'. And I think there's thirteen of 'em."

Davvers nodded thoughtfully. "Well, there's certainly a few. We've two here, the Hopi have a number." He frowned. "There is another…now where did I read about that?"

"But gather 'em for what? What do I with them? And why me, I'm quite happy 'ere."

Davvers glanced at him.

24

"You sure about that, Tom. You implied yesterday that you were bored senseless. This sounds like a nifty little adventure to me."

"Well, you do it then."

"But I'm not the chosen one, Tom."

Tom sat with his thoughts. Yes, I'm bored. Bored with a monotonous seaside town, bored with school, bored with the same routine, fed up with Mum nagging and Dad moaning about making ends meet.

Davvers broke the silence.

"Thing is, Tom, you obviously have a connection with the skulls. They're communicating. These voices are telling you things. If this keeps happening, you may discover what they seek. But, for now, do you believe what you've seen, what you've heard? Do you believe in the power of the skulls?" He leaned forward and looked at Tom in earnest. "Do you believe it's possible the legend is real, that you are the chosen one?"

Tom glanced across at Jack, who looked at him anxiously. A nifty adventure or bored senseless. When he said bored, he just wanted a bit more happening here, not some weird talking skull. But deep down he wanted to know – he wanted to know what it meant. He looked at Davvers.

"I wanna believe, but it's difficult."

"Psh, psh," Zannor ranted as he appeared from nowhere.

Jack almost choked on his cake.

Zannor's fingers twitched in anticipation as his eyes sought out the skulls. Davvers picked them up but Zannor shook his head angrily and pointed at Tom.

"The chosen one, the chosen one."

Tom swallowed hard.

"Psh, psh, the crystal skulls, protect, protect, I protect." He prodded Davvers and pointed to Tom. Davvers hesitantly handed Tom the skulls.

"I think you need to give these to him."

"But they're ours."

Zannor ranted, deranged. "Protect! I protect!"

Jack sat rigid and Tom's heart thumped as he stood up and took the skulls from Davvers. He slowly held them out to Zannor. The hermit stepped forward.

"Flipping heck," Jack muttered.

The hermit walked through Tom's arms. Tom grimaced as he saw the skulls floating inside Zannor. He let go and pulled his hands away in disgust.

"Psh, psh, the halls...the halls of antiquity, take it, take it." The crystal began dissolving. Within seconds Zannor had absorbed them and faded into the sandy wall. Tom quickly wiped his hands down his shorts and glared at Davvers.

"He's taken 'em! Where's he taken 'em?"

"Of course!" Davvers rushed to the back of the cave, rummaged through a pile of papers and, with a triumphant cheer, returned to Tom and Jack with a pamphlet clutched in his hand.

"The halls of antiquity. That's what I've always called..."

He unfolded the leaflet and laid it on the ground. Tom and Jack moved forward as Davvers picked up a long wooden stick and pointed at sections of the leaflet.

"This is a floor plan of the British Museum in London. That's where I read it, there's another skull there."

"Gather me in," Tom muttered, "take me, the halls of antiquity."

His heart skipped as he looked at Jack in horror.

"They're telling me I've gotta steal that skull."

CHAPTER SIX

In the beach café, Tom looked anxiously at Jack.

"I can't just walk into a museum and take it. I'm already on thin ice. Mum and Dad 'ave had a right go about me bunking off school and now this. How am I gonna afford to get to London? And what happens if I get the skull?"

He shook his head in frustration. Why couldn't Davvers be the chosen one? He seemed more cut out for adventures.

"Hang on, let's think about this logically," Jack said. "What're the visions about? Is there a theme? Is everything connected?"

Tom felt in his pocket and handed Jack a small notebook.

"I've written everything down. All of this has happened since I found the skull. I shouldn't believe any of it; I wouldn't if it hadn't have happened to me. So, unless I'm going completely mad…"

He glanced at Jack, who flicked through the book.

"Earthquakes, floods, tornadoes…well, it's weather but not much to go on." He put the book down. "Look, I may not see your visions, but I saw those skulls disappear in that bloke's stomach and that was enough for me. There's something weird going on. What're you gonna do?"

Tom looked out at a dead-end town with dead-end jobs. The chosen one, that's what the skull had said. Descendant from those that made 'em. That old man in the dream – transcend any doubt, he'd said. He felt his heart race as he looked at Jack.

"Will you come?"

Jack put his head in his hands. "I knew you'd ask that."

Tom could almost hear the cogs turning in Jack's brain. He knew he was asking a lot of his friend, who studied hard and had already planned his life. Jack flicked through the notebook, stared out of the window and rubbed his forehead. He took a deep breath and slumped back in his seat.

"Yeah, I will, but we better have one heck of a plan. We're gonna have to lie, cheat, steal. This isn't nicking sweets off a counter, this is walking into the British Museum and taking an ancient artefact."

Tom bit his lip and nodded. He could hear the judge now: 'Yes, M'lord, Mr Carver pinched the skull because they speak to him.' Transcend any doubt. That's easier said then done. He looked at Jack.

"We'll go to London. If it looks too dodgy, we'll just come home."

Jack grinned. "We're still gonna need one heck of a plan."

"Well, I've got an idea. D'you think Davvers has still got his army uniform?"

***

Sunday morning, Tom plonked on the sofa eating a bacon sandwich, and flicked through a book on Native Americans that Davvers had loaned him. Dad had the papers sprawled across the dining table. Mum stood in the doorway with a bowl of cereal.

"You left the grill on, Tom. You'll burn the house down one day. And don't forget to tidy your room, I'm sick of the mess."

Tom's eyes remained firmly on the book. "Don't go in there then, it's my room, I like it like that."

"The place needs a good clean."

"Don't answer your mum back," Dad said. "It's her one day off, she shouldn't have to be tidying up after you."

Tom gritted his teeth. Nag, nag, whinge, bloody whinge.

Why can't they work Sundays too? The doorbell rang. Tom took a deep breath as Mum went through to the hall.

"Wonder who that is?" she said. "Is Jack coming round?"

Tom mumbled that he wasn't but secretly prayed for everything to go well. He heard pleasantries exchanged. Mum had put on her telephone voice as she invited their visitor into the lounge.

"Do come through."

Their guest stepped in and Tom pressed his lips tight to stop from laughing. Davvers stood tall and impeccably dressed in military uniform. Tom hadn't seen him without his Panama hat before. He had thick dark hair, greying around the temples. He'd waxed his moustache and curled it up at the ends. It gave him a constant smile.

Every part of his uniform had been ironed to precision and Tom could see his reflection in his polished black shoes. His tunic had a variety of coloured ribbons and medals. He secured his peaked cap tightly under his left arm and, with his right hand, he gripped a shiny, wooden cane.

"Good morning," he bellowed. Tom's dad nearly spat out his beans as he leapt up, almost standing to attention. Mum wiped her hands on her apron.

"This is Brigadier Davenport, retired, of the Royal Marines." She looked at Tom. "You didn't tell me you knew a Brigadier, Tom."

Tom didn't know how Davvers would play this so he shrugged as Mum continued using her posh voice.

"Would you like to partake of breakfast, Brigadier?"

"You're too kind, madam, but no, I've already eaten. Completed a five mile jog this morning and breakfasted at 07:00 hours."

Tom suppressed a laugh as his dad stood more upright, holding his stomach in. Davvers continued, clearly enjoying his role.

29

"Thing is, Mr and Mrs Carver, I've been an awful nin-compoop. I arranged for some pupils to accompany me to Devonport tomorrow to have a look at the naval base there. Biggest naval base in Western Europe you know."

"Oooooh," Tom's mum exclaimed.

"Thing is, there were two youngsters that I seemed to have overlooked. That's young Tom here and his friend, Jack Newton. I know it's short notice and all that, but you don't mind if they tag along, do you? They'd be awfully disappointed if they couldn't come. As it's my fault they were missed, I'll let 'em come along for free."

Tom saw that Mum had fallen under Davvers' charm. "Well, yes, of course, it'd be a shame if they couldn't go, wouldn't it love?"

Dad, looking uncomfortable in the presence of an officer, mumbled his agreement.

Davvers whacked the wooden cane against his leg. "Jolly good. It's an overnight trip so make sure he's all packed. I'll pick him up tomorrow at 06:45 hours. All right?"

"Yes, yes, that's lovely. What d'you say, Tom?"

Tom, although silently delighted at the performance, remained visibly disinterested much to his mum's annoyance. Davvers gave her a brief smile.

"Good show. Tom can see me out. Delighted to meet you all."

He clicked his heels, saluted and marched out. Tom followed and gave Davvers the thumbs up as he opened the front door.

"Davvers, the rail tickets. I can't pay you back yet."

"Like I said when we first met, don't judge me on appearances. Six forty-five, Tom Carver, the quest begins."

CHAPTER SEVEN

Tom, Jack and Davvers stood on a forecourt and gazed across at the towering grey pillars of the British Museum. Behind them, a coach arrived, where a party of school children and three harassed teachers got off. Tom met Jack's smile as the children dispersed, with the teachers' constant nagging. "Put all your sweet wrappers in the bin," "Try and keep together," "Don't wander off," "If you get lost, come back to reception." The voices faded as they disappeared inside. Davvers shuddered.

"My goodness, what a rabble. In my day, we had two straight lines. Boys on the right, girls on the left. No sweets, no chance of getting lost."

Tom grinned. "When was that then, the 1800s?"

"Steady on, Tom."

Tom shoved his hands in his pockets. "This is good news for us."

"How?" Jack said.

"A party of kids, no uniform. Perfect cover. We'll join up with 'em."

Jack frowned. "Look, I don't know anything about stealing but surely it'd be better if no one was about."

"No! Jack, it'll make sense to tag along with 'em. The more people there are, the more chaos there'll be."

"And if there's chaos, no one's gonna know what's going on."

"That's right." Tom put his rucksack on. "Right, you both know what you're doing?"

Jack and Davvers nodded as they made their way up the steps and through the entrance. The cool marble interior washed the summer heat away.

Davvers went to pay for maps and guide books and Tom and Jack wandered about. The immense rooms echoed with hushed whispers and soft footsteps. History oozed from every corner, Greek gods gazed heavenward, faded tapestries of Persia hung from the walls, but Tom couldn't warm to any of it. Dead stuff. What's the point of looking at dead stuff?

A whisper swept through the corridors.

"Clannah khall clanni sha."

Tom tensed. Jack looked at him.

"Clannah khall clanni sha."

Tom took a deep breath as Jack rushed up to him.

"What's the matter?" he whispered.

"It's the skull. It knows we're here, Jack. It knows we're here."

Davvers joined them.

"Everything all right?"

Jack grabbed Davvers' arm. "Did you hear it?"

"What?"

"The skull!"

Davvers looked disappointed. "No, no I didn't."

Tom felt a bit sorry for him. He clearly wanted this more than him. Tom nudged them.

"Come on, those kids are going upstairs."

They followed the group and, although it all seemed pretty dull, Tom and Jack perked up at the displays in the Egyptology room. Tom recognised things he'd seen in Davvers' cave.

Colourful vases; tall, pompous looking cats; flat palettes with all manner of gods carved on them; huge chunks of limestone etched with hieroglyphics; models of mummies and sacred cows. Tom stuck his head in an open sarcophagus where the dead would have been placed. The children gathered around, mimicking.

"Look, remember that film, The Mummy."

Tom and Jack laughed along until one of the teachers told them all to quieten down and announced that it was time to visit the Americas section.

Tom nudged Jack. "That's our bit."

He looked for Davvers. As instructed, Davvers meandered in the background pretending to be a tourist. He looked it too, with his guide book, studious look and Panama hat.

When they reached the Americas section, Tom stared in disbelief. He'd never been to America or shown the slightest interest in Native Americans but as his gaze rested on the exhibits, it all seemed extraordinarily familiar.

Bearskin robes, feathered headdresses, long thin tobacco pipes covered in white furs and tassels, rattles filled with maize kernels, bows and arrows, knives, and medicine. His head throbbed.

"Clannah khall clanni sha. Clannah khall clanni sha. Clannah khall clanni sha."

Tom covered his ears and staggered back. Jack pulled him to one side as Davvers joined them.

"What's up old chap?"

"It won't stop chanting – it's in my head the whole time."

Tom looked at Jack's worried expression; why couldn't he hear it? Davvers rested his hand on Tom's shoulder.

"Try asking it to stop. Talk back, tell it that you're here. Just think it."

Tom closed his eyes tight and concentrated. I'm here, I can hear you, please be quiet, I'll find you.

"Clannah khall clanni sha," it whispered gently and stopped.

Tom opened his eyes in surprise. "It listened. It's stopped."

33

"Thank goodness for that." Davvers slapped him on the back and wandered away.

Jack pulled Tom back. "There's a security guard at the back and cameras in two corners."

Tom looked around. "Yeah, I know. Davvers'll distract him. I'll just 'ave to face away from the cameras. I'll put me hood up."

Further along, Tom scanned every part of the room. He grabbed Jack's arm.

"Look over there. In the corner."

Jack glanced across. Standing on a black plinth, under a Perspex case, stood the crystal skull. It dominated Tom's vision. His eyelids drooped as he walked hypnotically through the crowd. It whispered gently. Tom sent his thoughts out. I'm near now. Make this easy for me. Please don't let me get caught.

As he reached the skull, a museum guide gathered a group of people around. Tom snapped out of his daydream and blended in with the crowd. The guide put his hand on the Perspex case.

"Legend says that the skulls have some sort of power. The Hopi tribe in the southwest of the United States tell us there are thirteen skulls in total."

Tom's ears pricked up. He moved forward and raised his hand.

"What're they for?"

The guide looked grateful for some interest. "Well, they say that if all thirteen are brought together, it's supposed to help bring about the survival of the human race." He smiled at his audience. "A little over the top, I think."

Tom smiled but a shiver ran through him. "Where're the other skulls?"

"Well, we've obviously got one here. The Native Americans have some. An explorer from the British Army has one."

Tom nodded knowingly. "So have all thirteen been found?"

The guide shook his head confidently. "No. We know there's four missing. The Hopi claim to know where they are but they won't say."

"Where do the Hopi live?"

"Mainly Arizona."

"Well if it belongs to them why don't you let 'em have this one?"

"This was donated by the finder. We're not about to let this one go, seems quite a popular attraction."

Tom put his hands in his pockets, trying to stay calm but adrenalin surged through him like an express train.

"D'you know anything about the Fourth World?"

The guide raised his eyebrows. "Yes, yes I do. We're in the Fourth World now. That's all part of the legend. It's a bit of a long story for the quick tour but if you're about later, I can tell you a bit more." He looked at his watch. "But if there's no more questions, please follow me through to the next section."

As the tourists moved on, the guide glanced back at Tom and winked. "Let's hope the prophecies aren't true, eh?"

Tom looked at him quizzically. "Why?"

"Well according to the legend, the Fourth World ends in December 2012."

CHAPTER EIGHT

Tom turned to Jack. "Did you hear that?"

Jack could only nod.

"Arizona! We've hardly been out of Cornwall. How am I s'posed to get over there?"

Jack, gaping at the skull, shook his head slowly and tugged Tom's sleeve.

Tom looked at him. "What?"

"The screws, look."

Tom glanced down to see the screws rotating, freeing the casing from the plinth. He stared, unbelieving. It knows we're here. It's helping.

"It's time," Tom whispered.

Jack casually scratched the side of his head and moved away. Tom slipped his rucksack off and drew back the zip. His body tensed.

"Psh, psh. The time has come, the time has come."

Zannor appeared – ghostly, bounding around the room like a gazelle. At the same time, a dramatic yell, followed by a heart-wrenching moan, echoed through the room and Tom watched Davvers crash to the ground, clutching his chest. Jack yelled for help and everyone went forward. This was it. He put his hood up.

"Take it! Take it!" Zannor screeched.

Tom's eyes pleaded at him. Stop leaping about. His shaky fingers freed the screws and placed the casing on the floor. With a quick glance around the room, he grabbed the skull.

A searing pain shot through his ears.

He stood in the middle of a housing estate staring at chaos. Three police cars screeched to a halt and officers tumbled out and waded in to struggle with a group of residents, wrestling them aggressively to the ground.

Tom found it difficult to breathe. The air tasted stale, the gardens had been scorched dry, and an old lady lay unconscious on the pavement. Neighbours stepped over her to join the mob. An unmarked police car drew up and, to Tom's horror, a plain-clothes officer stepped out with a handgun. Tom turned his head, flinching, as the gun fired twice above his head. The residents stood back, glaring at the officer.

Looking through the group, Tom saw a standpipe and an overturned table with a frightened and bloody official kneeling on the ground. The man with the gun stood firm.

"Everyone form an orderly queue."

Tom shouted to the group. "There's an old lady here, she's fainted." No one seemed to hear him.

"Go to hell," a middle aged man shouted at the officer.

The mob egged one another on, crowding around the standpipe. Tom winced as two men began fighting. It snowballed into a rampage as people fell over themselves to reach the tap. Two more shots rang out and the police stormed in to protect the official. The rabble quietened and the man with the gun spoke.

"You are only permitted one ration of water each. Now form a queue. Everyone'll get their share."

Random voices shouted out. "How can we survive on that?" "I've got three kids, this won't go far enough," "We need more water," "My husband's ill, he needs more," "Let him die, save it for the healthy."

Shots fired out again and the crowd hushed.

"It's one ration only. If you have more now, there's less later. If you're ill, go to the hospital. Now form a queue. Anyone assaulting this official will be arrested."

The group reluctantly shuffled into a line and filed past the terrified official, who shakily filled their containers with water. Tom saw a policeman bend over the old lady. Glancing across to his colleague, he shook his head.

"Another one for the morgue, Guv."

The searing pain returned. Tom shut his eyes tight. When he opened them, he had the skull in his hands. Through his watery vision, he saw a crowd around Davvers, and Zannor flitting from corner to corner.

A weariness enveloped Tom but the near invisible Zannor raged at him. With some effort, Tom rammed the skull in his bag.

"Clannah khall clanni sha. Clannah khall clanni sha. Clannah khall clanni sha."

Nausea crept up as he mentally shouted at the skull. SHUT UP! SHUT UP! He watched as Zannor ran around hysterically, sticking his tongue out at the cameras. Davvers writhed on the floor. Jack. Where's Jack? Tom scanned the room desperately.

Beads of sweat trickled down his temples. Jack, where are you? His eyelids drooped and his legs buckled as his energy deserted him. Forcing his eyes open, Tom reeled as the room spun.

Jack raced across and took the rucksack from him. He felt Jack prop him up as they staggered out. Desperate to escape, Tom tried to run but Jack pulled him back.

"Don't draw attention. Just walk normally, like we're finished."

"We will be finished if we get caught. I feel awful, Jack, I had another vision."

"Come on, let's get out of here."

They stumbled down a wide staircase and came across a different set of exhibits. Tom pulled at Jack.

"This isn't the way! We'll have to go back. They'll see it's gone."

"Shut up. There must be another way. Come on, there's gotta be signs somewhere."

They moved more quickly now. Every corridor led to more exhibits and smaller rooms. Tom's legs turned to jelly as every ounce of stamina vanished.

"Jack, I've gotta get out, I've gotta get some air."

Jack pulled at him. "Here, this way."

He opened a door and they fell into a huge domed interior with a gift shop and café. Hundreds of people sauntered about. Tom slammed up against the wall, struggling to breathe.

"I can't do this. We're lost, they'll catch us."

He winced as another vision shot into his head. He cowered in a wet, muddy hole. The jawbone of a skull stuck out hideously.

"Clannah khall clanni sha. Across...across the ocean, the breath of Mother Earth. She breathes. The breath of Mother Earth, where the four meet. Corners of the earth. Kokapelli."

The message wrapped around his brain like treacle. He covered his ears.

"GO AWAY," he shouted as the pain shot him back to the museum.

A hush descended as people stared disapprovingly. Jack slammed him against the wall.

"Flipping heck, Tom. Get a grip."

Tom looked over Jack's shoulder in horror. Jack followed his gaze.

"Oh no, that's all we need."

A burly security guard marched up to them. Tom's hands turned cold and clammy as he clung on to Jack. If he didn't get some air soon, he'd throw up.

"You two. You on your own?"

Tom closed his eyes and shook his head.

"No," Jack said, "we're with a school party upstairs but we got lost. My friend's not feeling well. We just need to get outside, get some fresh air. Which way do we go?"

The guard stepped to one side and pointed to the opposite end of the room.

"No more shouting please."

Tom smiled feebly at the guard. He and Jack weaved their way across the marble floor and Tom glimpsed daylight through the glass doors. The room closed in as the skull whispered endlessly.

Tom broke free from Jack's grip and sprinted away. Ignoring Jack's muted pleas he crashed through the first set of doors, raced across the corridor and into the foyer. Daylight filtered through enticingly. He went to run but a pair of podgy hands held him tight.

"Not so fast, boy." The voice sounded familiar, but so sinister and out of place. Tom looked up.

"Mr Griffith!"

CHAPTER NINE

Tom cursed. What the hell's he doing here? Griffith grabbed his ear and pulled him close.

"Take me for some sort of fool, do you, boy? I don't know who this Davenport fellow is but he didn't fool me. Oh no. I check things out. Especially when my most frequent truant is involved. Checked it out I did, and what do you think I found out about the brigadier. Not a lot. So, he's unlikely to be one, is he? A brigadier I mean."

Tom tensed. Griffith appeared almost vicious and his hands shook uncontrollably. A mild, hysterical laugh bubbled up as his fat face turned purple with rage. His eyes glared unnaturally, like a demon had crawled inside and possessed him.

"I've got you now, haven't I? Oh yes. You've given me a hard time since the day I started, but I'll show you. I'll get my revenge, don't you worry. You and that fake brigadier."

Tom squirmed. "He's not a fake, I've seen articles about him."

"All lies, the lot of it. A nobody, that's what he is. Like you. Your parents are waiting for you by the way, Carver. They're wondering what you're up to. Stole the money to get here, I expect."

The hysterics rippled through him again and Tom tried to wriggle free.

"You're seriously mental, Griffith. You must be a right perve, following me to London."

Griffith twisted his ear further but Tom managed to turn and grabbed his wrist.

"I COULD HAVE YOU UP FOR ASSAULT, YOU KNOW."

Visitors stopped and stared. Griffith released his grip, put his hand on Tom's shoulder and let out an embarrassed laugh.

"He's a one, isn't he," he announced, "always running off, the little rascal."

It placated those around them. Griffith leaned forward menacingly.

"You won't be so clever when I get the truancy officer to you, boy. Oh no, I'll make sure of it. You'll not be attending my school again. I'd rather kill you than 'ave you back. All the grief you put me through."

"Yeah right, and I'll press charges for assault if you don't let me go."

Tom rubbed his ear. Behind Griffith, he saw Jack running toward them holding Tom's rucksack. As he closed in, Jack swung the bag behind him and whacked it into the back of Griffith's knees. Griffith buckled and crashed to the floor, his chubby hands grabbed his fat legs as staff ran across to help. Jack pulled Tom away and they dashed through the main doors.

"This way," Tom ordered. They ran to the far end of the building and hid behind the last grey pillar gasping for breath.

Tom rested his head back on the concrete pillar then peered back toward the entrance. Two security guards came out and looked around the forecourt but, with a quick shrug, returned to reception. He glanced at Jack.

"I can't believe you did that. Did you see him? He's a complete nutcase. His face was as red as a monkey's bum."

Jack shook his head. "I don't know what I was thinking. D'you think he saw me?"

A man's shadow crossed them. They grabbed their stuff but a familiar voice chirped.

"Hello chaps," said Davvers, "thought I'd lost you. Everything go to plan?"

Tom dragged him behind the pillar and told him about Griffith. Davvers sculptured his moustache thoughtfully.

"Fancy him following you up here. That's a bit strange, don't you think? Is he still in there?"

"Never mind that," said Tom, "we're in deep trouble thanks to you."

"Steady on, Tom. You asked me for help, remember?" He gestured at the rucksack. "Have you got it?"

Tom glared at him.

"I'm in for a brilliant time. Griffith's gonna make my life hell, and enjoy it. I might even be expelled; he's already said as much, and all you can think about is that poxy skull. I've prob'ly been caught on camera, I'll prob'ly get arrested. Why the hell did I agree to this?"

Davvers gave Jack some money. "Get us all a drink, Jack, we'll wait here."

Davvers sat down on the concrete steps. "Tom, I didn't do well at school, never there much. Always wanted to be out exploring and discovering things for myself. Oh, I got into trouble now and again but it never stopped me from achieving what I wanted to achieve."

Tom stared ahead. "Well what's that gotta do with me?"

"There's one thing my parents taught me, Tom, and it's an important lesson. Always do the right thing, they said. Even if it turns out to be a mistake. If you think you did the right thing at the time, then that's all you can ask of yourself."

Tom chewed his lip.

"Thing is, Tom. You have to ask yourself that very question. I mean, weigh it up. The most extraordinary things you've experienced in the last few days. The skulls appear to be leading you onto some sort of quest. If they are…well, then you have a unique opportunity: an opportunity that no other

43

person has. So ask yourself, and be true to yourself. Did you do the right thing?"

Tom didn't have to think. The skull had spoken again; it was clearly doing something and he had to find out what. He looked at Davvers and nodded.

"Yeah, I did do the right thing."

"Well then, when you get home, take your punishment like a man, then pick yourself up and carry on."

Jack arrived with cold drinks and Tom gulped his down gratefully. The coolness hit the back of his throat and swept through him like a cold shower. He looked up at the clear blue sky and, without thinking, quoted words that had locked onto him like a magnet.

"Across…across the ocean, the breath of Mother Earth. She breathes. The breath of Mother Earth, where four meet. Corners of the earth. Kokapelli."

Davvers' eyebrows raised. "Kokapelli?"

Tom nodded. "D'you know where that is?"

Davvers stroked his moustache. "Not where – who! Kokapelli is a Hopi god."

Jack nearly choked on his drink. "That guide went on about Hopi legends."

Tom gazed at the sky, smiling.

"The next skull. It's buried."

"Where?" asked Jack.

"Arizona."

***

Tom sat on the bed listening to his mum. He fiddled awkwardly with his ring, wishing she'd shut up and leave him alone.

"I don't know what's got into you, Tom, I really don't, you're so moody just lately. The way you spoke to Mr Griffith, well it's just plain rude. And who's this army fellow if he's not in the army? Running about with a complete stranger, it's not how your dad and me brought you up."

Tom gritted his teeth. "He was in the army, he's retired, he's an explorer; I've known him for ages. He can't be a stranger if I know him, can he?"

As his mum continued nagging, Tom thought back to what Davvers had told them on the train back from London.

"The skull I found changed me. I'm a wealthy man with a wealthy background. Looked forward to a comfy retirement in Berkshire. Had it all planned. But the moment I touched that skull, something happened. I retired, sold up to live on a beach in Cornwall. I got all environmental, bought a boat for Greenpeace, financed a conference for Friends of the Earth, that sort of thing, and it's all since I placed my hands on that damned skull."

He leaned forward.

"Don't you think it's strange that our paths have crossed? That I suddenly decide to give everything up to live on this beach – the beach where you found another skull. What are the odds of that happening? What are the odds of Zannor leading you to me? Our paths were meant to cross. I believe you have a quest to bring the skulls together. You've been chosen, you're the connection. Now, I can't do much, Tom, but I can finance you. I can pay for your tickets to America."

Tom looked through Mum as she continued nagging. The skulls are alive! But where's it leading? And what's the quest for? He looked up at the ceiling. When am I gonna get some straight answers?

Mum glared at him with her arms folded.

"You haven't listened to a word I've said, have you? Not a word. Well, you'll stay up here until your dad gets home. He'll have something to say. And you'll go to school tomorrow. I'll take you there myself. Even though I've gotta take time off work, which we can ill afford." She stormed out.

Tom contemplated his plans. He'd asked Davvers to buy their plane tickets and talk to his Hopi friend, Ed. He hoped Ed would know more about the legend. He and Jack arranged to meet at 2am on Saturday. He picked up his mobile and dialled. The caller answered.

"Jack?"

"Tom, you all right? What did your folks say?"

"Doesn't matter does it, we're going soon."

The line went quiet.

"Jack, what's up?"

"I feel rotten, lying to Mum and Dad. I've never done anything like this before, have you?"

Tom rested his head on his pillow. "No. I know I've skived off and stuff, but nothing like this. I feel a bit empty about it all."

"Maybe we should say something."

"No! We're not to tell anyone. They'll think I'm insane. And I'll have to involve Davvers. They'll think he's some crazy old man with battle fatigue. I don't wanna make it worse for him."

He rang off and buried his head in his hands, then kicked his trainers across the floor. Bloody quest. Why'd they have to pick me?

Staring out of the window, small waves lapped at the shore and herring gulls squawked high above the ocean. A group of builders walked along the sands eating fish and chips. They threw their wrappers and empty beer cans as they strolled. Tom threw open the window.

"YOU IDIOTS, PICK IT UP! LOOK WHAT YOU'VE DONE! YOU'RE SO STUPID, YOU RUIN EVERYTHING."

His stomach flipped. Where did that come from? His shouts carried back on the breeze and the men walked on. He glanced down at his rucksack.

With little motivation, he packed a holdall and tucked his passport and what little money he had inside. Jamming it under the bed, he sat down and looked at Davvers' Native American book and waited for Dad. He'd never seen Dad angry and knew he'd be a complete walkover. Promises, that's all it took. Go to school, do the chores and anything else they insist on. Easy.

But an empty feeling wormed its way into the pit of his stomach. The thought of sneaking out gnawed at his conscious. Leaving didn't seem right, not without saying something.

He sat up. I'll write a note. I'll write a note and that'll make it all right. At least they won't worry and they'll know I'm okay. His shoulders relaxed. Why hadn't he thought of it before?

With his mind at ease, Tom returned to his book. After two paragraphs, he scrambled for the phone.

"Jack, listen. I've got Davvers' book here. It mentions the Fourth World. Listen. The present Mayan age began in August 3114 BC and finishes in December 2012."

"Well, we know that."

"It talks about destruction and climate change and that mankind will cause this."

"Well, that ties in with your visions."

"But Jack, there's something I don't understand."

"What?"

"The Mayan lived for a thousand years. They recorded every astronomical event for hundreds of thousands of years before they even existed. They had exact dates for everything. The first three ages were calculated thousands of years before they existed. So they predicted all that time behind them and some time ahead."

"So?"

"Well, that's the problem. Just *some* time ahead. They don't go beyond 2012. Nothing's predicted after that date. If there's nothing else, Jack, then how can the quest succeed?"

CHAPTER TEN

Tom yanked his bike from the cycle sheds. What a week! The Express had run a small column about the theft of the skull and Tom almost fainted when he'd read it. Thank goodness they couldn't watch the CCTV. They'd blamed it on an electrical fault but Tom knew it was Zannor. Griffith, unfortunately, had got the same paper and pointed aggressively at Tom.

"It's you, boy! You did this and I'll prove it."

"Oh, stop your whining," Tom shouted back, "I'll sue you for slander and then you'll look a right idiot."

Griffith stomped away. Tom smirked as he cycled home. Mad as a box of frogs. Couldn't run a raffle, let alone a school.

***

On Friday evening, a transparent Zannor appeared in Tom's bedroom. Tom had to concentrate hard to see him. His faint bony hand pointed at the stolen skull. Tom pleaded with him.

"But what d'you want them for? Why can't I keep it?"

Zannor's weak voice rasped, "Protector. I protect."

Tom shook his head and sighed. "Well it's there, just take it."

Zannor stepped back, fearfully. "The chosen one, the chosen one."

Tom cocked his head. "What happens if you take it?"

"It will not come. I am not chosen. I protect."

Tom watched him closely. Judging by his reaction, something nasty would happen, so he picked up the skull and held it out. It dissolved, along with Zannor, into thin air.

As the skies darkened, he opened the window, hoping the cool breeze would keep him awake. Tom grimaced every time he checked his watch. The seconds ticked by slowly and he paced the room trying to think of anything but the task ahead.

At eleven o'clock, the stairs creaked. He put his ear to the door and listened as his mum and dad tiptoed across the landing to and from the bathroom. Finally, the lights went out and, within an hour, he heard Dad snoring.

After endless games of solitaire, Tom checked his holdall for a fifth time: passport, money. He looked at the clock and took a deep breath. Right, this is it. Zipping up his fleece, he checked his mobile, picked up his bag and glanced anxiously around the room. Tentatively, he turned the handle, opened the door and peered through the gap. All clear.

Creeping warily across the landing to the stairs, he checked the gap under Mum and Dad's door. So far, so good. He cringed at every step but gradually made his way down. The odd creak echoed up the stairs like a felled tree. He glanced up, expecting to see Mum there with her arms folded.

In the hallway, he offered up a silent thanks and listened for any movement. From the pocket of his jeans, he pulled out a creased envelope. It simply said 'To Mum and Dad'. He chewed his lip as he placed it under the telephone book. They shouldn't find it for a while. With a final glance back, he flicked the safety catch on the front door and left the security of home.

Once past the front gate, Tom raced through the shadows and down to the seafront. He dodged in and out of doorways as the odd car drove by. Sprinting across the promenade, he jumped onto the beach and saw Jack wave and disappear into the cave. Tom quickly joined them.

"You all right?" he said to Jack, who nodded apprehensively. "Have we got everything? You weren't followed or anything?"

Jack shook his head. He looked at Davvers. "You got the tickets?"

Davvers waved them at him.

Tom handed him a piece of paper. "Here, I printed off the directions to Heathrow."

"Excellent. The car's up on the road."

Jack grabbed Tom's arm. "What about our parents?"

Tom glared at him. "No! They're not to know."

Jack nodded, disheartened, and followed Tom out of the cave. Outside, Davvers closed the cave. By strategic placing of grass and driftwood, the entrance blended into the dunes. Tom shook his head in amazement. It was as if the cave didn't exist. They climbed onto the promenade where Davvers' car stood. Tom dropped his bag.

"Wow!"

He ran his hand along the pristine paintwork of a vintage Rolls Royce. He circled it, studying the huge round fog lamps fixed tightly to the shining chrome bumpers. The classic flying lady statue at the front of the bonnet gleamed in the moonlight. Peering through the windows, he saw worn, red leather seats and large, round dials on the dashboard.

Davvers threw the bags in the boot and opened the back door.

Jack clambered in ahead of Tom. "Blimey, Davvers, does this belong to you?"

Davvers made himself comfortable in the driving seat.

"Yes. Yes, it does. Got rid of the house but couldn't get rid of this. The lady who bakes my cakes keeps it in her garage."

Tom sunk into his seat and breathed in the smell of aged leather and musty oil. He stretched his legs out as Jack opened up shiny steel ash trays neatly fitted into the side panels. Walnut finishing and soft champagne-coloured carpets transported them to another era, an era of style and sophistication. A mass of polished dials and switches covered the dashboard like a 1940s spitfire. Tom nudged Jack.

"This must have cost the earth," he whispered.

Jack nodded enthusiastically.

"Family heirloom," Davvers said, "had a bit of inheritance from Ma and Pa and this was part of the will." He put the car in gear. "Chaps, you've a long day ahead – get yourself some sleep while it's still dark. There's travel blankets on the back shelf."

The Rolls glided like a feather on air. Once the novelty of the car had worn off, Jack covered himself with a tartan rug and immediately fell asleep. Tom tried closing his eyes but sleep wouldn't come. Careful not to disturb Jack, he climbed into the passenger seat. Davvers glanced at him.

"Tom, you really should get some sleep."

"I will, but I need to ask you something."

"Ask away old chap."

"Davvers, the Mayan didn't see beyond 2012. What's the point in all of this if the world ends on that date?"

Davvers raised his eyebrows. "How do you know it's going to end? Did your book tell you that?"

"Well…no, but…"

"Let me ask you something. Do you believe everything you read?"

Tom sat back. "If it's a history book I do, but not always a newspaper. They don't always tell the truth, do they?"

Davvers smiled. "Well, it's the same in history books too. You see, Tom, history has a history of changing." Tom screwed his face up. "What I mean is, history is having to be constantly re-written."

"But once somethin's happened, it's happened; you can't change it."

"No, you're wrong. There are lots of things being discovered by scientists and geologists as new technology comes in. A few years ago, some chap dug up a cave man from a glacier. Because of our technology, we discovered more about him in an hour then any anthropologist would have done a generation prior. What he wore, how he hunted, even what his last meal was. One thousand years ago, we believed the earth was flat and then someone discovered it wasn't. D'you see?"

Tom nodded. "So just because the Mayan couldn't see beyond 2012, it don't mean to say that's the end."

"That's right. The Hopi see beyond that date. The earth's gone through three traumatic worlds, there's no reason why it can't survive the fourth."

Tom watched the motorway lights whiz by in a blur.

"Davvers? If you were in my shoes, would you be doing this? You know, going on a quest."

"Most definitely. But it's not me, it's you. Tom, if you want me to turn back, I will."

Tom reclined his seat and closed his eyes but sleep wouldn't come.

***

Heathrow Airport heaved with a mass of rude, intolerant people, but Davvers cut through the crowds with ease. A man in a black suit and sunglasses knocked Tom to one side.

"Watch it, you idiot!" Tom shouted, but the man had gone. He caught up with Davvers and Jack. "This place is pants."

Jack agreed but Davvers took little notice as he strode up to a check-in desk manned by a surly agent.

"Where are you travelling to?" she said.

"Los Angeles," Davvers replied.

"How many bags are you checking in?"

"None, just hand luggage."

She tapped aggressively on her computer.

"You're Charles Clive Bartholomew Davenport?"

"That's correct."

"Can you confirm who's meeting them the other end?"

"Ed Satowa."

Tom glanced at Jack. What's she mean, who's meeting them?

Davvers continued. "I believe they have access to the First Class lounge, is that correct?"

The check-in agent sneered and handed Davvers a piece of card.

"They must behave, it's full of businessmen."

"Young lady, don't judge everyone by your own standards."

Tom smirked. Well done, Davvers. The agent handed Davvers some documents.

"They're in Row 6A and C, boarding is at 10am and the gate number is 32. Directions to the lounge are on the back of the card." She sneered at Tom and Jack. "Have a good flight."

As they moved away, Davvers strode ahead, pinpointing a place to sit down. Jack pulled Tom back.

"Isn't he coming with us?"

"He must be! Maybe he's on a later flight or somethin'. Come on."

They raced to join Davvers, who had commandeered a long, wooden bench. He handed Tom and Jack several documents.

"Listen up and don't interrupt. These are your boarding cards. You won't get on the plane without them so keep them safe. Here are your passports. These are your return tickets. These are forms to fill in before you land. The crew will help you so don't worry."

Tom took everything. "What about you?"

Davvers looked at him and gave him one more piece of paper.

"This is the person meeting you at Los Angeles. He should be holding a board up with your names on it."

Tom swallowed hard. "What about you?"

He felt Jack slide up as Davvers continued.

"If, for any reason, he's not there, the airline staff will call the number they have for him. He's promised me he'll be there."

Tom took the paper. "You're not coming, are you?"

Davvers let out a huge sigh. "I can't."

A sense of betrayal bubbled up inside Tom.

"Yes you can, you're loaded, you're not just gonna dump us on this plane and let us get on with it. We don't know what we're supposed to be doing or where we're supposed to go…"

"Tom," Davvers said firmly, "I can't go because I'm not allowed to fly. I have a medical condition that prevents me from flying. Well, long haul anyway. The person collecting you is a man who will know people that can help you." He then puffed out his chest and announced proudly, "I'm off to Southampton."

"Southampton!"

"I may not be able to fly to America, but I can sail and I'm not missing out on what these skulls are about. I'm getting a crossing tomorrow. I'll keep in touch with Ed and see where I can meet up with you." He looked at his watch. "You boys really should make the most of the First Class lounge."

Tom and Jack trudged along to the security point where Davvers gave each of them a wallet.

"There's some cash there. I'll pay Ed for anything you need to buy."

Tom stared at the floor. This should be a journey of adventure and discovery, but without Davvers, his anxieties had returned with a vengeance. Davvers shook Jack's hand.

"Good luck, Jack Newton. Look after your friend here."

Jack smiled nervously. "I will."

Davvers ruffled Tom's hair, and shook his hand warmly. "Good luck, Tom Carver. Do yourself proud."

Tom forced a smile. "I'll do my best."

In the luxury of the First Class lounge, Tom fell into a dream. He stood on a pavement opposite a huge convention centre. Across the road, a man in a black suit and sunglasses pointed a gun at him.

CHAPTER ELEVEN

The immense 747 rolled down the runway and heaved itself up into the skies, slowly and assuredly climbing higher and higher. Tom watched London fall away and the city gave way to green fields, towns and, finally, the Atlantic. On board, Tom and Jack sunk into their sumptuous First Class seats.

"Wow, this is fantastic," Jack said, opening a magazine. "There's films, TV shows, loads of games."

The crew handed out menus and Tom ordered chicken curry with rice. He swallowed hard. Chicken curry. That's what Mum and Dad like. His nerves turned to guilt as he stared out of the window. They'd have found his letter by now. He could picture it all.

Mum would be pacing up and down and Dad would read the letter he'd left:

Dear Mum and Dad,
Please don't worry, I'm completely safe. It's just that I've been given a very important job to do and it's only me that can do it.
I can't tell you where I'm going otherwise I won't be able to fulfil my quest. Jack's with me and we'll try and keep in touch so that you won't worry.
I know you're probably very angry but I think you will be extremely proud of me, and Jack, because I can't do this without him. Davvers is with us and is making sure that we are okay and safe.
Love
Tom

He could visualise what followed. Mum would be blaming Dad, who'd stand there soaking it up like a sponge. They'd make a cup of tea and Dad would call friends and neighbours and discover that no one had the slightest idea of their whereabouts.

Mum would blame Davvers. Tom rolled his eyes. I hope they don't think he's some weirdo. He came to the conclusion that they probably would. He could hear Mum on the phone now.

"Constable, this man has abducted two boys. Filling their heads with some rubbish about a quest."

Tom chewed his lip as his heart thumped. The police would be involved. There'd be a huge search party. Mum would be wringing her hands and Dad might actually get angry. Jack took his headphones off.

"Tom. I didn't tell you before because I thought you'd get cross."

"What?"

"I left a note for my parents."

Tom sat up. "So did I."

Jack's shoulders dropped in relief. "I couldn't just go without saying anything. It didn't seem fair."

"You didn't say where we were going."

Jack glared. "Course not. I'm not stupid."

"Sorry. It's just that…I don't like saying it but I don't want 'em to find us. Not yet anyway. Does that make sense?"

Jack nodded and put his headphones back on.

After dinner, Tom reclined his seat and snuggled under a duvet. Within seconds, he fell into a vivid dream.

The sun's rays warmed the early morning chill. Tom turned his nose up at a discarded barrel of used oil. Filthy black liquid had poured across the gravel and killed the plants and shrubs in its path. Empty cans and sandwich wrappers overflowed from the litterbin and blew across a deserted car park.

57

He wandered across to a low level, glass fronted building. Above the doorway was a sign: 'Visitors Centre, open 10am-7pm'.

In the window display he saw Kachina dolls, similar to those Davvers had. One, in particular, stood out. It looked so ordinary, dressed in dirty white cotton trousers and a floral tunic with beads around its neck. The face had been painted a reddish brown and a frayed, red bandana completed his outfit.

Tom brushed the hair from his eyes and gasped. The doll had moved! He peered through the glass. Must have bendy joints. He shrugged, but checked one last time before leaving the centre and walking along a marked path.

The odd small bird flitted through the pale blue sky. Tiny lizards scuttled in and out of small rocks. Cottontail rabbits scampered in the distance and crickets chirped noisily. At the end of the path he saw a wooden bench that overlooked a shallow valley. He sat down and gazed at a vista that, for some peculiar reason, seemed familiar.

Natural sculptures, battered by a thousand winters, created huge red rock arches that rose high above the ground. In the distance he thought he saw Native Americans with long spears but, in a blink, they'd gone. Unwanted questions bombarded him. When will you return? Why destroy me? Why treat me this way? An uninvited wave of resentment set in as a familiar, husky voice startled him.

"Your thoughts, they are more in common with the red man than the pale face."

Tom stared at the man beside him. The Native American from his dream! His eyes drew Tom like a magnet. They held a lifetime of history; wisdom glinted from them like a gold nugget nestled in a hundred pebbles.

"Where did you come from?"

"I have watched you many times."

"I dreamt about you before."

"I have appeared often. You look but do not see. You follow our beliefs, marvel at our lands, yet you do not speak."

"But I don't know anyone, I've never been 'ere before."

He smiled. "You visit many times – in your dreams. But like all dreams, they fade on waking. You speak to our spirits when you visit. Our people hear you. They walk this land. They know your destiny. To help our Mother Earth."

Tom stared, unblinking. Is he talking about the quest? His shoulders sagged at the thought of it. How do I do this on my own?

The Indian spoke. "One person's kindness can send a ripple across the globe. A powerful leader is just one man. You are just one man, you will achieve great things."

"A powerful leader can do what he wants."

"So many leaders but they continue their path. Trample our lands, destroy our earth and the animals on it. What have leaders achieved since taking our land?"

Anger pummelled into Tom. Who were they to replace land with concrete, poison rivers and run animals and tribes to extinction? He looked at the man.

"They've done plenty," Tom said sarcastically. "Plenty of suffering, pollution, lies." He kicked the ground.

The old man rested his hand on Tom's arm. "Do not harm the earth in your anger. Channel your aggression. You have much to learn."

Tom stood up and faced him. "Channel it where? What am I supposed to be doin'? If this is a dream, why don't I wake up? How could I 'ave been 'ere before?"

The old man rose and beckoned Tom down a steep slope.

"Come. It is time to take something from your time among us. It will help with your quest."

Tom stumbled after him. "You know about the quest?"

Tom followed him down an uneven track littered with

stones and rocks. The old man walked with ease, almost gliding over the surface. His rasping voice chanted a tribal song.

"My song speaks of the buffalo," he said as he finally stopped and listened. Tom stood alongside him.

"What're you listening for?"

"Your mind is impatient. You will hear it first. Then you will feel it. Then you will see it."

Tom gazed across the prairie, slowly becoming aware of a rumbling. The noise increased, the vibration in his chest felt like someone banging enormous timpani drums right beside him. The ground began shaking, trembling, and Tom sidled up to the old man, who raised his arms heavenward.

Then Tom saw it.

Huge clouds of dust rose up on the horizon as the earth rumbled beneath them. His heart leapt as his senses were bombarded with buffalo. Thousand upon thousand of gigantic black beasts stampeded across the prairie, their hooves creating a red fog as far as the eye could see. The smell of animal and earth filled the air and Tom whooped and laughed.

"WHERE DID THEY COME FROM?"

"The past," the old man replied as he walked on. Tom jogged after him. The herd ran across the plains and into the distance. The crescendo died down and he caught up with the old man.

"What d'you mean, the past?"

"It is good to see this land before the settlers. When man and nature lived together." His hand gestured to the plains.

Tom stepped back at the unfolding panorama. A village of tepees appeared along the riverbank. Wispy smoke carried with it the smell of corn and fry bread. Buffalo grazed in the valley; young children played tag, men returned from hunting and women sewed and cooked. The elders sat in discussion, debating and talking. Horses, dogs and goats stood silently beneath the trees.

"Come."

The man led him into the camp where the tribe welcomed them warmly. He guided Tom to a group of three men who had gathered around a recently killed buffalo. Tom couldn't help but feel sorry for the animal, its dead eyes lifeless and forlorn.

"Do not be sad," the old man said, "we use everything. Nothing is wasted. Every piece of the buffalo is used for something. We have big ritual; it is a very sacred animal. We offer prayers and song to help replenish the herd. We worship all animals. From one thousand buffalo, we kill only one. From one thousand whales, the Eskimo kill only one. Come."

The old man led him to a quieter area where they stood by a hole, the size of a manhole cover. He knelt and put his head into it. Tom looked on quizzically.

The man knelt back and beckoned Tom to do the same. Tom knelt beside him and, with some trepidation, leaned into the hole. A rush of wind enveloped him and he breathed in the clearest and purest air he'd ever known. Only the aching of his spine forced him to kneel back.

The old man smiled and pre-empted Tom's question.

"This is the breath of Mother Earth. She has been breathing since the dawn of time. This is our past."

His hands went skyward and he began chanting in Navajo. Tom didn't know how he knew this, he just did. The old man rested back, looking tired now, but gestured for Tom to experience it again. Tom eagerly put his head back in.

But this time it was different. A mild breeze flopped his hair about. The air, although fresh, didn't seem so pure. Tom leaned back and looked at the old man who, again, pre-empted him.

"Mankind has taken so much from her and they give little back." His voice became emotional. "The breath of our Mother

Earth becomes shallow. She is sick. Why is man so consumed with destroying her with his greed and power?"

His passion overwhelmed Tom, who blinked back his own tears.

"You are learning," the old man said as he rose and retraced his steps. "One person can make a difference. Be sure not to let the emotion stay in your veins. Let it flow through you like a river to the sea. Take the lesson – pursue the future."

Tom scrambled after him. "I will help. I'll do my best. Are you gonna help me find the skulls?"

"Follow your heart. You mourn the actions of people who destroy, but we mourn our Mother, the Earth. You will not be alone."

He wandered on. He looked so ordinary in his white trousers, floral shirt and frayed red bandana, and yet beneath his slight frame Tom knew he walked with a powerful man.

They reached the main path and, in the distance, the community that Tom had witnessed began fading in the sun's haze.

"My ancestors return to their Father Sky. You will find your destiny. We will be near. Now sit and be at one with us. Look to the sky."

"What?"

"Look to the sky."

As Tom looked up, the sky darkened and he witnessed a vision that would stay with him forever. Tens of thousands of tribal people wound their way along an invisible pathway into the skies: Navajo, Apache, Sioux, Cherokee, Seminoles walked side-by-side with animals and birds – a huge river of souls took their place in the heavens, and became remote sparkling stars of the galaxy.

Tom squinted as the sun took the vision away. He sat alone in the high sierra. The desolate breeze whistled past his ears and the red rock arches stood majestically above him.

Returning to the Visitor's Centre, Tom stopped, transfixed. There, on the pathway, stood the plain Indian Kachina, dressed in a floral shirt and frayed red bandana. The barrel of oil had been sealed tight and the scattered litter had disappeared. Tom picked up the doll.

"Tom?"

His vision blurred, he staggered, disorientated; his shoulders began shaking. He jumped out of his dream and found Jack standing over him.

"Tom, you okay?"

He nodded, his face full of wonder.

"I've had the most amazing dream but…it didn't feel like a dream. I was there. I know it sounds daft."

Jack shook his head. "No, mate, I'm still blown away by that Zannor bloke so nothing sounds daft to me. What's that?"

Tom looked down and gasped.

He held the Kachina in his hands. A flimsy piece of brown-tinged paper slipped out from its tunic. Tom unfolded it. Jack leaned across.

"What's it say?"

"The keepers of earth may perish and become a myth, but this world shall swarm with the invisible dead of their people. At night, they will gather to pray for our Mother Earth that you are so keen to destroy. You must deal kindly with Mother Earth or she will exact revenge. The dead are not altogether powerless."

CHAPTER TWELVE

At Los Angeles, a young man in a battered straw cowboy hat stood grinning amiably.

"Hey, dudes. My name's Ed. You're Tom and Jack, right?"

Tom nodded. He'd assumed Ed would be the same age as Davvers but Ed must have been about twenty. He looked pretty cool in his baggy jeans and a denim shirt.

"Okay, who's who?"

"I'm Tom Carver and this is Jack Newton."

Ed smiled. "Hey, love the accent. Welcome to LA. Now let's get outta here."

He set off at such a pace, Tom and Jack had to jog to keep up, but after a few minutes, they arrived at the Cherokee Charters desk. Ed smiled at the check-in lady.

"Hey Marilyn. This is Tom and Jack. We've gotta plane for Gallup, New Mexico."

"You sure have. It's ready and waiting, and we need you out there pretty quick."

Tom glanced anxiously at her.

"What's up?" Ed said.

"The British police know their passports are gone, it's just a matter of time before they find out where they're headed."

"Flippin' heck," Jack said.

Tom's stomach flipped. He looked at Ed fearfully.

"Hey, don't worry, dude. They may track you to LA but they'll stumble for a while. This is a big country."

The knot in Tom's stomach loosened. Ed was calm personified. Tom couldn't imagine him getting flustered. No wonder Davvers trusted him. Ed held up their tickets.

"Anyway, this is my pa's airline and we're using Indian names." He handed them their boarding cards. "Tom, you're Distant Eagle and Jack, you're Loyal Coyote. Like 'em?"

Tom and Jack grinned in approval as Ed ushered them through the terminal and onto a small Cessna plane. In no time, they had taken off and Tom and Jack tucked into lemonade and peanuts. Tom sank back and looked at Ed.

"Where're we going?"

"Gallup. It's a small town in New Mexico. Run by Navajo, Hopi, Zuni – it's out in the high desert. The air's fresh, the food's good and the natives are friendly." Ed flashed a smile at them.

"Are you a native?" Jack asked.

"I'm Hopi. We're from New Mexico and Arizona. Our people have been here for thousands of years."

The pilot shouted back to them.

"Hey, Ed. Message for you, put your headphones on."

Ed made his way to the cockpit. Tom tried to eavesdrop but the engines drowned out any hope. But it wasn't long before Ed returned.

"Your cops are good. They've already tracked you to LA."

Tom spilled his drink. "What!"

"Hey, chill dude, they'll take some time to find where we're heading. They'll get our cops onto it. Your folks are heading over tomorrow."

The knot in Tom's stomach returned. "But they'll find us. Cherokee Charters, they'll say something."

Ed eased back in his chair with a smirk.

"No way, dude. I told you. It's my pa's airline. Marilyn's my sister and Cherokee are packed and gone. By the time they figure it out, we'll have disappeared. Like I told you, you're gonna take some finding."

He lifted a can and raised a silent toast. Tom tried to look unconcerned but anxiety gnawed at him. *Mum and Dad must be frantic. And the police! We'll get deported and locked up, and all for chasing myths and legends.* He glanced up as the pilot shouted back again.

"One more message. Someone else is on your tail. A Mr Griffith."

Tom stared at Jack.

"Hey, dudes, who's Mr Griffith?"

Tom could barely answer. "Our head teacher."

"Wow. He must think a lot of you."

Jack let out a laugh but Tom stared at the floor uneasily. *Teachers don't pursue pupils half way across the world. Why's he following us?*

CHAPTER THIRTEEN

Tom and Jack sat on a tatty sofa in Ed's sparse flat where a group of Native Americans had gathered. They occasionally glanced at them and spoke quietly to Ed using their native Navajo. Tom scowled. Ed turned and smiled.

"Tom. These guys are Navajo elders. They're more comfortable speaking Navajo. They hope it doesn't offend you."

Tom silently cursed himself and quickly smiled back. "Sorry. I just wondered what you were saying."

"They're saying to rest up for a few days. They know about the quest."

Tom's eyes opened wide. "How?"

"They're Shamans, medicine men. They have visions, dreams. The legends belong to our people, we knew it was coming."

"Will they help me find the skulls?"

"No. The skulls only speak to the chosen one, but we'll help where we can."

Tom slumped back as Ed continued.

"Our people won't betray the skulls. They're part of us. We've been waiting for the legend to rise and send its message."

"What message?"

"To put mankind back on the right path."

A newfound confidence filtered through Tom. If these medicine men believe in the skulls, there has to be some truth there.

***

On the morning of the third day, Tom and Jack sat on a bench by the cultural centre waiting for the advertised Hoop Dance to begin. A few tourists joined them on seats scattered around the square.

Tom wiped the sweat from his brow and looked down the road at the small stores selling locally made rugs and jewellery. Jack opened a bottle of water.

"D'you think we're gonna be here long?"

Tom leaned back. "I hope not. I wanna get on now–"

Ed waved frantically from across the road. Tom grabbed his rucksack.

"Something's up."

They sprinted across to him.

"What's wrong?"

"Visitors. Follow me and stay close."

They jogged, single file, down a narrow alley and, at the other end, Ed stopped and pushed Tom and Jack into a bricked recess. He took his Stetson off and leaned against the wall in front of them. Tom strained to see.

"What's happening?" he whispered.

"Ssshhh."

They leaned back, held their breath and heard the rumble of a car engine. A police officer leaned out of his patrol car.

"Hey, Ed. You seen two boys 'round here? They're fourteen years old, come from England. Both tall and lean. One with blond hair, the other's dark brown."

"Ain't seen anyone. You try the hotels down the street?"

"My partner's onto that. If you see 'em, their parents are here. Just tell 'em to report to the station."

Ed nodded thoughtfully and watched the car drive off. Tom and Jack let out a huge sigh and waited for the all clear. Tom peered around the corner and watched the black and white patrol car turn and disappear. They scampered across the road to the Thunderbird Café, an empty '50s diner, where the owner ushered them upstairs to a stark room overlooking the main street. Ed stood in the doorway.

"Listen, dudes, I'm heading back to my place to pack your stuff. We'll head out to my grandpa. He's about an hour away in Arizona. Steve's downstairs in the café. If you want anything just make sure you're not seen. See you later."

Tom nodded and looked out of the window to see two more patrol cars cruise by. He watched as the officers stopped to ask questions and hold up photographs. He hoped no one recognised them from the cultural centre.

"Jeez!" Jack dived to one side, pulling Tom along with him. Clouds of dust rose up as Tom wrestled him away.

"What're you doin'?"

Jack screwed his face up, pointing to the street below. Tom peeked down and caught his breath. Their parents stood immediately beneath them. He slid the window up an inch.

"Well, they couldn't have gone far," Tom's dad said. "I mean, it's small, it's miles from anywhere. They're complete strangers, someone must've seen them."

"That's right," Jack's dad replied, "they'll stand out like a sore thumb."

Mum sounded frantic.

"Well, why can't we find them? This is absolutely ridiculous. What on earth are they doing out here anyway? What's so important that they have to come all the way out here? And why couldn't they tell us?"

Jack's mum chipped in. "It's that army bloke that I'm suspicious about. Someone must have seen him. Even in a suit, they'd recognise that moustache. Never liked moustaches. Make you look suspicious, even when you're not."

Jack rolled his eyes. Tom smiled and continued listening.

"Maybe he shaved it off," his dad said. "He does seem to have vanished though. But he wasn't on that plane, was he? They came over on their own."

Jack's mum blew her nose. "What if we don't find them?"

The loud, booming voice of Mr Griffith interrupted them.

"What's he doing here?" Tom whispered to Jack, who looked equally perplexed.

"Ah, there you are. Thought I'd lost you, I did."

Tom's dad swung round.

"Mr Griffith, why are you here? This isn't a school matter. Are you ill?"

"Ah yes, no, well, you see, I'm not having it. All this truancy and lip I get. He's been off school more times than you've had hot dinners, oh yes. No, I'm not standing for it. It's my holidays now, you can't stop me taking a holiday. Always fancied coming here. Kill two birds I can. When I get hold of him–"

"This isn't the time. Can't you see we're all anxious about their safety. Go home, bloody interfering baboon."

Tom smirked. Jack's mum opened the café door.

"Oh, let's go in here and think about what to do."

Tom took out his mobile phone but Jack stopped him.

"Don't use that! They might trace the call."

Tom tutted. "But we have to warn Ed."

"How?"

The stairs creaked. He pushed Jack and they quickly shuffled behind the sofa. Tom closed his eyes as the door creaked open. Steve popped his head in.

"Hey. I've got some English people in so don't come down."

"They're our parents," Tom whispered.

Steve came in and closed the door. "Shoot! They're ordering food. I'll call Ed, get him to pick you up some place else. This is too close."

"Where? And how do we get out?"

"There's a fire exit at the bottom of the stairs where the bathrooms are. Go through there, turn left and carry on to the Grizzly Bear Bookshop. Ed'll pick you up there. Say twenty minutes."

Tom nodded. The plan seemed okay until he trod on the first stair. The crack sounded like a bomb going off. Jack closed his eyes and Tom sent up a silent prayer. In the café, he heard muffled conversations. He glanced at Jack and gestured for them to carry on. The jukebox sprung noisily to life. Seizing their opportunity, they tiptoed down the stairs. Half way down, the door leading to the café opened and Tom's dad walked through.

CHAPTER FOURTEEN

They froze. One glance and they'd be seen. Tom almost collapsed in relief as he watched Dad open the toilet door and go in. He nudged Jack.

"Come on," he mouthed.

They reached the bottom of the stairs where the engaged sign flipped to vacant. The door opened with Tom and Jack behind it. Tom's heart skipped a beat as the door opened wide. This is it, he's gonna see us. Another hand held it open and Tom almost fainted in relief when he heard Steve's voice.

"Food's all done." He ushered Dad through to the café, winked at the boys and closed the door behind them.

Jack's face blended with the white-washed walls. "Flippin' heck, that was close."

"Come on," Tom said, opening the fire exit. "Let's get out of here."

***

Huddled underneath old tarpaulin in Ed's rusty pick-up truck, Tom heaved. The stench of grease and oil, coupled with the heat and motion, played with Tom's stomach like a food mixer.

"Jack, I think I'm gonna be sick."

"Oh no, don't throw up here. Lift this up a bit."

Jack pulled the tarpaulin up and warm air filtered through. Tom took a few deep breaths while Jack poured a bottle of water over his head. He peered over the tailboard and saw the town disappear over the horizon. Ed turned off into a lay-by.

"Hey, dudes. Come on out now." He stripped the tarpaulin away and found Tom and Jack sweltering underneath. "Sorry guys. Had to make sure you weren't seen."

Sitting up front with Ed, Tom opened the window and breathed in the fresh air.

"Where're we going?" Tom said.

"We're gonna stay with my grandpa on a reservation up at Four Corners."

"Four corners!"

"Yeah, you heard of it?"

Tom nodded eagerly. "Where four meet. Four corners."

"The message!" Jack enthused. "That's what the skulls said."

"What is Four Corners?" Tom asked.

"It's a place where four states meet. New Mexico, Colorado, Utah and Arizona. There's a monument up there and an Indian market."

"Is that where Mother Earth breathes?"

Ed gave him a quizzical look. "Now, there you've got me. Gramps may know, he's old, follows tradition, knows a lot of the old ways."

Ed continued driving down the empty road, pointing out sacred places and their meanings. Tom noticed that many stories involved Mother Earth and Father Sky. Everything, animate and inanimate, seemed to have a purpose or meaning.

He pressed his face against the window and gazed at the biggest sky he'd ever seen.

Ed turned off the highway and onto a dirt track. The truck bumped and rolled and Tom saw half a dozen decrepit caravans in the distance with some Pinto horses grazing nearby. Small shrubs and low, flat trees scattered the landscape. Beside each caravan was a round, clay dwelling. A hogan, Ed called it.

"My grandpa has a trailer but he prefers the hogan. A lot of our elders ain't so keen on square homes. The Indian belief always forms a circle. You know, the circle of life, the turning seasons, time. He sleeps on the earth, only wears shoes if he has to. That way he's in touch with Mother Earth. The doors face east so the sun's the first thing that enters. Each part of the hogan represents a different thing; reasoning, philosophy, life – that sort of thing."

"What about those?" Tom pointed at some that had been destroyed.

"Those belong to elders who've died. Their belongings go into the hogan and we burn everything."

Tom frowned. "Don't you inherit it?"

Ed laughed.

"No way. It's not ours to take. Traditionally, we've never been interested in anything but what we need. When the settlers arrived back in the 1800s, they just wanted gold, silver, and furs. Kept taking and taking. Still do, I guess. That's why people don't connect anymore. When you meet Gramps, you should ask him to show you. How to connect."

Tom nodded but didn't really know what he meant.

Ed parked the truck alongside a long, white trailer and they stood outside the hogan for some time. Tom shuffled on his feet for what seemed an eternity. He stuffed his hands in his pockets.

"Aren't we going inside?" Tom said.

"Once Grandpa's ready, he'll come out. We wait outside until they're ready. He'll have heard us. It's polite to wait 'til you're asked."

There was movement inside the hogan. An elderly man shouted out.

"Ya at eeh."

Ed smiled. "Hey Gramps."

The old man had to stoop to get through the arched opening of the hogan. He brushed himself down, straightened up and walked toward them.

"Ya at eeh," he said.

Tom stood transfixed. Dressed in dirty white trousers, a floral shirt and a frayed red bandana, Tom stared at the old man from his dreams.

"Ya at eeh, Tom. Hello Tom."

Ed's smile lit up his face. "Tom, this is Gramps. Chief Satowa."

CHAPTER FIFTEEN

Ed discreetly led Jack away. Tom looked at Chief Satowa with his craggy face and watery brown eyes. Again, he sensed a powerful figure behind the small frame, yet a sense of mutual respect existed that Tom couldn't explain. Taking Ed's advice, Tom made the first move.

"Ed said something about connecting."

Chief Satowa nodded knowingly and beckoned him to a shaded area where the horses grazed. He sat cross-legged, inviting Tom to do the same.

"I will call you Grandson. When you are ready, I am Grandfather. We are all related. Take off your shoes, let your flesh feel the earth."

Tom slipped off his trainers and waited. Satowa took a deep breath and sat silently for two or three minutes. It seemed a lifetime to Tom.

"Quiet time, Tom, people have forgotten quiet time. When did your mother last listen to nature?"

Tom screwed his face up. What an odd thing to ask. He shrugged. All he could remember her doing was nagging.

"Dunno. She's really busy, works full time at a supermarket and when she's home, well, she's always cooking and ironing and stuff."

Satowa picked up a handful of earth and placed it in Tom's hands. He spoke gently and assuredly as he gazed into the trees.

"This earth provides life. Mother Earth nurtures all. Our own mothers and grandmothers bring life to this planet, they give life to our children, they nurture, feed us and keep us warm. All women are sacred." Tom let the granules of dry mud slip through his fingers. "Your mother should reconnect. Listen."

Tom listened, unsure of what he was listening for. He stared intensely at the ground, hoping it would improve his hearing.

"I don't hear anything," he whispered.

"Close your senses to vision."

Tom shuffled to get comfortable, shut his eyes and listened. At first he heard nothing. But then sounds began seeping through.

The trickle of a nearby stream flowed gently with the clear waters from a far-off mountain; birds twittered, whistled and chatted among themselves; unseen wings fluttered in the trees; insects buzzed; horses whinnied, their hooves padding the ground. As the noises became familiar, Tom opened up other senses. He felt the sun's warmth on his arms and a gentle breeze flowing around them. He breathed in juniper and sage, sweet aromas of the high desert.

Another deep breath and he suddenly wanted this to last forever. Now he understood the elder sitting beside him.

He'd connected; this is Mother Earth, nature. No mobiles, music or cars; the constant hum of society had been banished from this place.

Chief Satowa began singing a gentle melody in his native tongue. Tom sensed something approach. A twig snapped. He opened his eyes and caught his breath, then shifted closer to Satowa. A stocky mountain lion crouched a few feet in front of them.

Satowa placed a reassuring hand on his arm. The lion kept its distance and glared suspiciously at Tom. Satowa stopped singing and spoke in Navajo. Tom watched the animal stroll toward Satowa like an old friend, nuzzling him, enjoying the

77

fondling and fussing. The lion's animosity to Tom softened and he sat with his head in Tom's lap.

"Is he yours?" Tom said, looking at Satowa in admiration.

Satowa shook his head. "I have known brother lion since he was born. I knew his mother and grandmother. We sit together often under this shade."

"But he's so tame."

"We are old friends and friends have no need to be afraid in each other's company. I have told him that you are my friend so he will treat you the same. He is confused. It is unusual for one of your kind to be so friendly. He fears the men and their guns. His mother was killed just three summers ago in such a way."

"Why?"

Satowa shook his head sadly. "They did not need her. They were not hungry, they had no need for clothing. It was a senseless kill and left this little one without his mother."

Tom understood his message. He remembered the vision of the buffalo that he'd shared with the chief. Why take something you don't need? Why kill animals you don't need?

"How does he understand you?"

"That, my friend, I do not understand myself. The Great Spirit connects us all. Words do not travel. We speak more through gestures and vision."

Tom leaned in and gently hugged the lion. Its fur felt like thick velvet and its eyes melted his heart. He gazed into them – they had the same wisdom as Chief Satowa – as if they knew everything. The lion sauntered away.

"You connect well, my grandson. When you sit with your mother, take her to nature."

"I will."

He wished Mum were here now. She would have loved this. He smiled at Satowa.

"Grandfather, in my dream, you showed me where the earth breathes."

Satowa closed his eyes and smiled.

***

That evening, the four of them sat in Satowa's rusty trailer and ate a delicious home made lamb stew. Tom tore off a piece of fry bread.

"Excuse me Chief Sa... Grandfather, are we staying with you for a while?"

He nodded slowly.

Jack leaned forward. "Are you a real chief, with a headdress and stuff?"

Tom almost choked. "Jack, that's old hat, you're thinking about the 1800s."

"Well, I don't know, do I? I'm only asking."

Chief Satowa smiled at them. "Yes, Jack, I am, although it has little meaning now. When younger, I remember differently. Now, it is ceremony."

Tom pushed his plate back. "Grandfather, how did you get into my dream?"

He waved the question aside. "The message is more important. You will see more visions."

Tom sat back, unsure as to whether he wanted to see more. Most of the visions hadn't been pleasant at all.

Jack chipped in. "Are the messages part of the quest?"

The old man smiled and pulled his chair closer.

"I am a Shaman. I have visions that help heal. I pray to the Great Spirit. The spirit comes to me in visions, shows me where to gather the plants that will heal. The visions that Tom sees are important to him. To his quest."

"But I don't understand half of it, it's in riddles," Tom said.

"Then you must solve them, learn from them."

"I think the skulls are showing me the future."

The chief smiled. "Only you know. But you have a wise mind, Grandson. Remember, they link for a reason, only you have their trust."

"What is the legend?"

"There are thirteen skulls. They will gather to bring a message. Hopi belief says mankind always has a choice. There are two paths for every decision. Hopi believe mankind has taken the path of materialism, technology, greed. He is now separate from nature, separate from the Great Spirit and sadness has entered his heart."

"And the skulls will put this right?"

Satowa's expression gave nothing away. "We will only know if the thirteen are gathered."

"But why am I the chosen one? Why not a Hopi?"

"Only you will know. You will discover these things on your journey."

The chief leaned forward and rested his arms on the small table in front of him.

"But I can help you with one thing. Tomorrow, you go to where the earth breathes."

Ed spread out a map and Tom studied it closely as the young man pointed to certain areas.

"Okay, dudes. We're here, Navajo reservation. To the north are hills, but before this, there's grassland."

Ed handed him an object. "Can you use a compass?"

Tom nodded, taking the compass from him.

"Go north for four miles and you'll come to the back entrance of the National Park where you met Gramps in your vision. You'll see the Visitor's Centre in the distance."

The chief tapped Tom on the shoulder. "Your approach, it is from where you saw buffalo."

Tom nodded again. "I know where you mean. But where will the skull be?"

"You must trust your instinct, my grandson."

Tom's shoulders sagged. Instinct. The park looked about five miles square. It could be anywhere. Ed got up and handed them some sleeping bags from the cupboard.

"It's getting late, you need to rest. I'll wake you guys just before sunrise."

***

The following morning, after a crispy bacon sandwich, Tom and Jack began their walk to the park. Tom held Ed's compass firm, checking it constantly, holding their position. Jack kept his eye on his watch.

"If we keep to this speed, we'll be there in an hour," he said.

Neither boys said much. Immersed in their own thoughts, they watched the ground beneath them as each step took them closer. Tom thought about the legend and the Hopi beliefs. He looked up.

"There. In the distance. That's the Visitor's Centre."

They picked up the pace across the grass. Tom couldn't believe that millions of buffalo had once roamed here. Now, only the odd bird flew high above them. He looked across at Jack.

"Race yer."

They sprinted across the grass and the pale, desert landscape turned to rich brown. In two minutes, they'd arrived at the back entrance of the park. Catching their breath, Tom knew exactly where he was and led Jack across to the blowhole.

"Put your head in."

Jack looked suspicious but Tom urged him on. He knelt down and leaned in. Tom smiled – he could hear the breeze from where he stood.

Jack leaned back. "Flippin' heck."

Tom put his rucksack down. "Brilliant isn't it?"

"Flippin' heck," Jack repeated, staring at the hole. "This really is a living planet. It's not just things growing on it and living off it. It actually breathes."

Tom nodded and put his compass away.

"Clannah khall clanni sha," the skull whispered.

"Psh, psh, quick, quick, the time has come."

Zannor materialised and jumped up and down in his tatty brown robe.

"Psh, psh, hide, hide."

Tom flinched.

Zannor didn't normally say that! He looked across the plains and back toward the huge red rocks. He couldn't see anyone but Zannor continued shouting. Jack cocked an ear.

"Listen."

Tom screwed up his face. What is that? It sounded like rumbling but he felt no vibration.

"Psh, psh. Up. Up."

Tom looked up. In the distance, a black object came speeding toward them. Jack pushed Tom to the ground.

"HELICOPTER. HIDE!"

Jack slid into the blowhole. Tom threw his rucksack ahead and dived under a low shrub, his heart pounding. He stared nervously at the hole.

"Jack, are you all right?"

"Yes, I'm fine. I've found a ledge."

"I'll tell you when it's clear."

The whirring blades came lower and closer. It swept across the Visitor's Centre, then hovered over the main cliffs of the rocks, progressively getting nearer. The noise shattered the peace as the blades spun in a blur. Tom crouched low, hoping and praying they wouldn't be seen. The machine hovered above and dust flew around furiously. Tom peered up and saw a man in a black suit and sunglasses. Shrubs bent in the slipstream; he twisted his head away and closed his eyes to the dirt slamming into him. Then, as quickly as it had arrived, it moved away, across the plains, occasionally hovering above thick vegetation. Tom ran across to the blowhole.

"You okay?"

Jack nodded, gripping tightly to the rim. "I think so. Has it gone?"

Tom squinted in the early morning sun.

"I'm not sure what it's doing. Just seems to be sweeping an area."

Then, to his horror, it swooped around.

"It's coming back!"

As he scampered under the shrubs he heard Jack yell – a yell drowned out by the helicopter blades as it flew directly overhead and away into the distance.

Zannor reappeared. "Psh, psh. Quick, quick."

Tom brushed past Zannor, but when he got to the hole, Jack had disappeared.

CHAPTER SIXTEEN

"Jack? Jack, can you hear me?"

"Yes. I gashed my arm pretty bad though."

Tom looked around in desperation. Damn it! He laid flat and reached down into the darkness.

"Can you grab my hand?"

He heard Jack strain and scramble. His flailing hand appeared, but Tom couldn't reach.

"It's no good, I'll have to climb in."

"There's a sort of natural ledge about three foot down."

"Okay."

Gently manoeuvring himself into the blowhole, his feet scraped the sides, feeling for a foothold. Jack coughed and spluttered as stone and rubble fell away.

"Sorry mate. I'm just tryin' to get secure."

Jack spat dirt out as Tom edged down.

"Clannah khall clanni sha."

"AAAH!" Tom slid a few inches. A huge skull protruded from the mud.

"What is it?" Jack said.

Tom chuckled nervously. "It's the skull, it's here."

"Clannah khall clanni sha."

"Okay, I know where you are. I've gotta get Jack before I get you."

The skull obediently quietened as Tom made himself secure.

"Jack, I'm gonna reach down with one hand. Grab my wrist

and I'll grab yours. You get a firmer grip that way. Which arm are you using?"

"My right."

"Okay." Pushing himself against the earth, he stretched down. Their hands passed each other clumsily but then connected. Gripping tightly, Tom grabbed hold of the ledge above him.

"Right, on the count of three. One. Two. Three…"

Tom heaved as Jack scrambled and levered himself up. Stones and dirt fell down the hole as Jack kicked and scurried furiously. Tom heard Jack groan with pain but, after some desperate clamouring, he eventually found himself staring at Tom's chest. Jack let out a relieved sigh.

"I don't know how far down that goes, but I haven't heard any of those stones reach the bottom yet."

Tom glanced down, preferring not to think about it. "How's your arm?"

"I don't think it's broken but it feels like a deep cut."

Tom looked up.

"Jack, that helicopter went but I don't know if it saw us. We should get out and get back to Satowa."

"Where's the skull?"

He nodded to Jack, who twisted round and gawped at the skull behind him. He studied it carefully.

"They don't look so scary after a while."

"They do when come leapin' out of the mud."

"Clannah khall clanni sha. Palaces in the sky. Palaces in the sky. Green table, green table, Anasazi."

"Psh, psh. Come, come." Zannor hopped impatiently above.

The skull loosened and virtually fell into Tom's hands. The now familiar pain shot through his head. He felt Jack support him.

"Tom, what's the matter? Tom?" His voice faded.

Tom stood on a balcony overlooking an immense arena lined with thousands of soldiers. Alongside, stood high-ranking officers, their medals gleaming in the sun.

Coloured banners and statues bore the image of the man beside him. Tom sneezed and then almost collapsed in relief as he realised that no one could see or hear him. He made his way down to the arena.

Teenage soldiers struggled with heavy guns, as they sang an unfamiliar anthem. He saw no pride in their eyes, only fear. Some refused to sing, but one look from the officers changed their minds.

The ground rumbled. To his left, thousands of iron-grey tanks rolled into the square. Hundreds of long range guns followed behind.

Enormous black triangular aircraft gathered above, their forms casting dark shadows across the square. Tom squinted at a date on the banners. It was a foreign language but the year filled him with horror – 2012!

A pain flashed through him and took his sight.

"GET DOWN," a voice bellowed.

Instinctively, Tom ducked. As his sight returned, he found himself ankle deep in mud alongside young men in ill-fitting uniforms and tin helmets, their faces haunted by the visions of war.

Tom didn't need to ask where he was. He'd seen it on the History Channel. The First World War – the rat infested trenches of the Somme.

But TV didn't prepare him for this. Decomposing bodies half buried in sludge littered the walkways. Muddy streams trickled blood red through the trenches as grown men whimpered like children. The air made him retch, the smell of death clung to the living like a disease.

Tom peered over the top to no man's land. Barbed wire

rolled for as far as he could see. Young men gasped and reached for masks as invisible mustard gas crept over the rim. Tom coughed; his lungs burned as he wiped his streaming eyes.

A bomb exploded within a few feet; the power pummelled into him and punched so hard that he felt every bone in his body had splintered. He writhed in the mud and spat blood. A young soldier stepped through him to his colleague.

"Weeks they said. Been 'ere months. Whole flaming village gone. Who's gonna do the harvest when we get back?"

His friend stood motionless with dead eyes.

"Just us now and you're away with the fairies." He lit a cigarette and put it in his friend's mouth. "But if you can walk, you can fight. That's what the officer says."

"OVER THE TOP IN ONE MINUTE," the officer ordered.

The men lined up. An eerie silence descended – an ominous quiet as if everyone knew their fate. Tom tried to shake the soldier but his hand simply slid through him.

"Don't do it, you'll just die, thousands of you will die."

Oblivious to Tom's pleas, the soldier put a pistol in his friend's hand then prepared his own rifle.

"Goodbye Mum, Dad. Give me and Eddie's love to Beth and Gertie. We would've made handsome couples, that's for sure." He nudged his comrade. "And you'd have been a brilliant uncle."

Tom gasped. They were brothers! The soldier put his helmet on, pulled out a creased photo and kissed it.

"Cheerio sweetheart."

A shrill whistle sounded. The brothers clambered over the top. Deafening shots and explosions knocked Tom down like a dead tree. Every shattering boom kicked the breath from his lungs. He dragged himself up a rickety wooden ladder.

The brothers lay dead.

Tears welled as he grabbed hold of the fluttering photo.

"NOOOOOOOOO…" The trench collapsed on itself and sucked Tom down among the rats.

"TOM! TOM!"

Tom opened his eyes wide; mud-stained tears fell as he sobbed uncontrollably. He collapsed onto Jack, who struggled to keep them from plunging into the bowels of the earth.

"Tom. Listen to me. I don't know what happened but you're back. I'm here, I'll stay with you, the visions can't hurt you."

"Why did they make 'em?" Tom spluttered between sobs. "The earth, I felt it, Jack. Every bomb ripped her open. She was in agony."

As fast as Tom brushed away his tears, more came. Jack pushed him up.

"I can't hold you much longer."

Tom nodded, took some deep breaths and focussed. Jack nudged him again.

"We've got to move. Hand the skull up."

Tom squinted up at Zannor, who leapt and twitched in the daylight. He manoeuvred the skull up and watched it dissolve as Zannor faded from view. Jack pulled him back.

"The skull's safe. Stand on the ledge and wait here 'til you're okay."

Tom stared in horror as the sticky mud appeared to close in on him. He kicked out frantically.

"I've gotta get out of here."

He pulled himself up. Jack scrambled behind. In the sunlight, Tom flopped cross-legged on the dirt and put his head in his hands. Jack sat alongside.

"I'm here mate. It's okay now."

Tom stared at the photo of Gertie and fought back the emotion that consumed him. What a waste. A whole generation wasted. And these brothers, they couldn't have been much older than him and Jack. Gertie's face smiled back at him.

Wonder what happened to her. He closed his eyes, thankful to be out of the trench.

But his relief was short lived as a pair of hands grabbed them roughly from behind and bundled them headlong into the back of an old green car.

CHAPTER SEVENTEEN

They fought to untangle themselves as the car bounced across the desert. Tom eventually grabbed the passenger seat and sat forward.

"LET US GO."

The man in the seat turned.

"Hey dude, relax."

"Ed!"

Jack finally stopped rolling about and grabbed the back of the driver's seat.

"What's the big idea, bundling us like that?"

"Sorry dudes. We saw the 'copter, thought we better come and get ya. This is my cousin. Doesn't do much talking. Just drives."

"I don't think they saw us," Tom said, looking questioningly at Jack.

"Well, I ain't taking chances. Gramps is waiting up ahead." He frowned at Tom. "Hey, you okay?"

Tom slumped back and closed his eyes.

"He had another vision," Jack said. "I think it was pretty bad."

Ed mumbled to his cousin and the car sped up.

"Best we get outta here," he said.

"Where to?" Jack said. "We don't know where the next skull is."

Tom whispered, almost trance-like, "Palaces in the sky. Palaces in the sky. Green table, green table, Anasazi." He opened his eyes and looked at Ed's raised eyebrows.

"Anasazi. They're the ancient ones, an old tribe. The Hopi and the Navajo are descended from the Anasazi."

Tom welcomed the news. "Well, where did they live?"

"All over. They had cliff dwellings. Way up high."

Jack leaned forward. "It's gotta be one of those places. What else did you say? Green table? Is there a place called Green Table?"

Ed and his cousin exchanged glances and shook their heads. Tom slumped back as Ed grabbed Jack's arm.

"Hey, what's this?"

Jack turned his arm over and Tom winced at the deep gash oozing blood.

"We'll get Gramps to look at that. Step on it, Cousin."

The car bounced across the desert, away from roads and civilisation. Tom held on tightly as they regularly became airborne before crashing back down again. He searched the sky for helicopters and wondered how long the car would last – both bumpers had been torn off and the boot sprung up and down at every invitation.

After a few bone-crunching miles, they turned onto a tarmac road where Chief Satowa waited with Ed's truck. After a hasty transfer, Ed drove off and Satowa opened a small wooden box of herbs and pieces of bark. He sprinkled them over Jack's bleeding arm.

"This will discourage infection, take away soreness."

He then looked at Tom and cleared his hair away from his forehead. Tom knew he looked a mess.

"Your vision, it has scarred you."

Tom nodded wearily. "I was in the Somme. The western front. Every explosion felt like my insides were being blown up."

Satowa nodded thoughtfully. "You are connecting, Grandson."

"The skulls spoke but I don't know what it means."

"Have you got a map?" Jack said. "And is there any chance we can stop and eat? I'm starving." He looked at Tom. "And if he's going into a coma every time he touches those skulls, he'll need food."

"Pull over at Pontiac's." Chief Satowa said.

Pontiac turned out to be a café owner and, over a burger, they studied a map. Tom focussed on every detail, hoping the skulls would mystically guide him, but nothing happened. Satowa pointed to several places on the map.

"These are all ancient sites. Anasazi dwellings. Here, here. Here, and here."

Tom leaned in closely. "I can't see anything called Green Table. Maybe it's some sort of plateau."

"Could there be Anasazi stuff somewhere else?" Jack said.

Satowa nodded. "There are many places. Not just Arizona, but New Mexico and Colorado."

As the others ate, Tom examined every part of the map. It must be here somewhere. Taking a square at a time, he studied the finely printed place names. Suddenly, he slammed the table.

"There, that's it! It's been in front of us the whole time. Mesa Verde. It's a National Park in Colorado."

Jack screwed his face up. "Well, what's that supposed to mean?"

"Mesa Verde. That's Spanish for Green Table." He grinned at Jack. "See, I did go to some lessons at school."

They quickly gathered their belongings, bundled into the car and headed north.

***

Five tiring hours later and the long roads gave way to a steep drive of sharp bends and inclines that slowed them down to tortoise speed. The dry desert landscape gave way to tall pine trees that swayed in the summer breeze.

Ed pulled off to the side of the road. Ahead was the entrance to the National Park where a park ranger talked with a policeman.

"Great. Now what?"

"They are park police," Satowa said, "but we take no chance, Grandson." He pointed to a dirt track behind them. "Head up, we will walk down."

Ed drove off road and parked in the shade of some pine trees high above the park entrance. Tom got out, breathed in the fresh pine air and stretched off. Satowa held Jack's arm. The blood still seeped out. He studied the ground.

"Tom, please, collect some daisies."

"Daisies!"

Satowa waved him away as he retrieved a small bowl from the truck. Tom looked around and reluctantly collected what there were.

"We're supposed to be looking for skulls, not poxy daisies."

Satowa called across. "Just the leaves."

Tom rolled his eyes and searched the grass. After a few minutes he returned to Satowa with a handful of leaves. Satowa placed them in a bowl, added a dash of water and ground the leaves with a stone. Tom looked across at Jack, who appeared just as bemused.

"What're you doing?" Tom asked.

"The leaves of the daisy help heal broken skin, reduce swelling, take out infection." With the leaves ground to cream, he applied it freely over Jack's arm and covered it with a piece of cotton. "Tonight, take this off, let the skin breathe." He looked at Tom. "You doubted me, Grandson."

Tom shuffled his feet. "I didn't mean to. I should know, shouldn't I?"

"Come."

Satowa gave him a reassuring smile, offered thanks for the leaves, then began making his way easily down a rocky path. Tom recalled how agile Satowa was in his dream, whereas he and Jack constantly tripped and lost their balance.

Satowa called back. "Let the earth guide you, focus on your destination."

Jack tutted but Tom focussed and became more steady on his feet. He looked for ruins but saw none. How could anyone build anything here? We're almost in the clouds!

After half a mile, Satowa stopped. Birds surfed on the thermals below. A wide valley gave way to endless miles of rich, green pasture. Tom scanned the horizon from right to left. The sight caught his breath. Two thousand feet above the valley floor, his eyes fell upon Mesa Verde.

"Bloody hell," Tom exclaimed. "There must be a hundred rooms there."

Built beneath the overhanging sandstone, the ancient Anasazi structure blended easily with the red cliff face. Although ruined, it stood out majestically and seemed as natural as the birds and the whistling breeze.

His knees trembled at the sheer drop below him. He'd seen parachutists jump from a lower height than this.

The ruins stood quietly, gracefully gazing across the valley as they would have done a thousand years ago. Tom imagined the view would have been the same – cliffs, trees, shrubs and farmland.

Satowa stood between the two boys and placed the palms of his hands on their heads.

Tom's head buzzed and the ruins transformed into life. Men made bricks from mud and water. Small fires flickered in doorways and women prepared food over the spitting smoke. Some stored crops and sharpened knives, others made pottery as children played and elderly men passed a pipe. Rope ladders hung from the cliff top above and animals grazed precariously close to the edge.

Satowa took his hands away and the scene faded to memory. Jack spun around.

"Wow, how d'you do that?"

For once, Satowa looked a little smug but, on seeing Tom smirk, he quickly reverted to the wise man Tom preferred.

"A recent vision. One thousand years."

"How far back do your visions go?" Tom said.

"Backwards, forwards, they come when they are needed."

They made their way down to the ruins. An Englishman picked up some sandstone and put it in his pocket. He shouted across to his wife.

"We'll put it in the garden, love."

Satowa tapped him on the shoulder. "My friend, take only your thoughts and memories."

The man's pale face flushed scarlet as he replaced the stone and chivvied his wife away. Tom smiled. Even he felt he'd intruded on something sacred.

Tom looked at Satowa and whispered, "So, where's the skull?"

"Trust your instinct."

Ed leaned on an iron railing.

"Too many folks, dude. Go hide in the ruins. We'll go to that platform, up the steps there. We'll prob'ly have to wait until the park closes."

Tom nodded confidently. "I'll know it's time when Zannor pitches up."

He led Jack across the ruins where they sat on a boulder and watched the activity around them. Tom grimaced.

"This place isn't the same with all these people here."

"I know, looks like Newquay on a bank holiday."

Tom let out an apprehensive laugh. He wanted to relax but a knot tightened in his stomach. What awful vision

95

would descend on him this time? Jack's finger followed an indentation in the rock.

"What d'you think's gonna happen when you've got these skulls?"

Tom shook his head. "Dunno."

"D'you think something awful's gonna happen?"

"I hope not."

A park ranger shouted from the steps.

"Park's closing in ten minutes. Appreciate it if you'd start making your way back to your vehicles please."

Tom put his rucksack on and he and Jack walked along the back wall and into a small square room with a doorway leading out to the front. From the shadows, they watched the last of the tourists disappear. The park ranger began one last check. The boys backed into the shadows as he passed by and returned up the steps.

Jack looked at his watch. "Let's leave it a few minutes. Just in case someone else comes down."

In the silence, Tom couldn't hear much, only the distant call of the birds that flew effortlessly, way down in the valley. The thick adobe walls made everything eerily quiet. Creeping outside, Jack moved to the cliff edge and looked down.

"Have you heard the skull yet?"

"No. I haven't heard Zannor either."

For the next hour, they searched each and every room. Tom called to the skull. Jack asked for Zannor to appear.

But nothing happened.

Ed's exaggerated cough sent alarm bells through Tom. They ducked behind a wall.

Peering over, he saw Ed and Satowa being asked to leave. Two policemen bounded down the steps. Tom yanked Jack into the ruins and they raced through the rooms, ducking under archways and diving through windows until he stopped dead and pulled Jack back. He dragged Jack up a rickety wooden ladder and into a tiny, dark recess. They leaned against the wall.

"Clannah khall clanni sha."

Tom stared at Jack. "The skull!"

"Where?"

"Here, somewhere."

"What about Zannor? Where's Zannor? He should be here."

Tom scrambled along, feeling the walls. "Well he's not, is he?"

Jack stopped him. "Ssshhhh."

Tom's gaze searched the dimly lit room, expecting the skull to jump out like it did before, but nothing happened. The police closed in. Muffled voices called their names. Tom panted heavily. It wouldn't be long before they found the ladder. The ladder!! Tom grabbed Jack.

"Pull the ladder up."

"They're too close, they'll hear us."

"TOM? JACK? COME ON, GUYS, WE KNOW YOU'RE HERE."

Tom pushed him.

"They'll find us anyway. But if they don't 'ave a ladder, we'll have more time."

Jack scurried across, got a firm hold of the top rung and began lifting the ladder. Three rungs up and Jack felt resistance.

"OK boys. We know you're up there. Get down here now."

Tom threw his head back in despair. *Zannor, where are you?*

Jack looked down at a stocky policeman in a leather jacket, his hand rested on a gun in his holster.

"Get down here, boy, and bring your friend with you."

As Jack lowered the ladder, Tom probed every brick in the wall, mumbling and pleading.

"Come on, where are you? You have to tell me where you are."

"Clannah khall clanni sha."

The now familiar blinding light seared through his head. He found himself in a bright open plan office in a tall skyscraper. The view through the floor to ceiling windows was blue; blue sky, blue sea. Buildings hugged the coastline and as he looked further along the shore, he saw futuristic structures that he recognised from travel brochures. Dubai! This is Dubai.

Seated around a large oval table, several executives argued with one other. On the table lay an architect's map and, as Tom got nearer, he could see the outline of plans to build out to sea. Looking out of the window, construction had already started. A large American man, smoking a foul smelling cigar, thumped the table with his fist.

"I ain't shelving a project for no fish," he roared. "We've invested too much into this, our shareholders will skin us alive."

"Monsieur, s'il vous plait, please."

Tom watched an animated young Frenchman get up and gesture for the American to quieten down.

"Monsieur, zis is not just fish. What you are proposing – it's preposterous." He pointed at the plans. "You cannot reclaim the sea 'ere. You'll destroy an entire coral reef that supports an extremely complex eco system. Thousands of rare fish, coral, vegetation. They support other species; giant turtles that 'ave been 'ere for 'undreds of years, and for what? 'Omes for rich footballers and people who 'ave nothing better to do with their money. Let them buy their 'omes inland."

"Listen, Frenchie, this is business. I have advanced deposits on every property out there. I've invested millions, and we stand to make millions so get your butt outta here. You're not even on this project."

The Frenchman held his hands up in defeat and began gathering his papers.

"Aah yes, of course, I was forgetting," he added sarcastically. "Everything with you, it comes down to money. Never mind about what we do to the ocean. I don't know 'ow you sleep at night."

Tom looked on sadly as he walked out. The American shouted after him, "Go preach your wacky ideas some place else." His business associates laughed politely.

"BUNCH OF IDIOTS," Tom screamed, but, of course, he knew they couldn't hear him.

The light flashed again and Tom sat, drained and dejected, in the darkness of the ruin. Jack raced to his side as the policeman reached the top of the ladder.

"Tom? Have you got it? Have you got the skull?"

"WHERE?" Tom shouted angrily. "WHERE IS IT?" He jumped as the policeman yelled at him.

"Boy, your time's up. Get down here. Now."

Tom bit his lip, fighting back the tears. With Jack's help, he made his way down the ladder. He looked at Jack and wearily shook his head. Jack kicked out at the policeman.

"Give him five more minutes, let us go for five minutes, we have to find it."

The officer whipped out his gun as his partner roughly tied restraints around Jack's wrists.

"You kick me again, I'll shoot you."

Tom pulled Jack back. "Leave it, Jack. There's nothing we can do. It's finished."

CHAPTER EIGHTEEN

Tom kicked his heels against the wooden chair and stared at the floor. He glanced around the Farmington sheriff's detention centre; a basic room with a desk, six chairs and a grubby lino floor. Through the barred window he could just make out a small field and some trees in the distance.

His mind raced, searching for answers. He'd heard the skull, seen the vision. Why didn't the skull appear? And where was Zannor? He got up and kicked a chair across the floor.

Jack stood up, shoved his hands in his pockets and wandered from one corner to the next, eventually stopping at the window to stare through the bars.

"We have to get out of here."

Tom let out a sarcastic laugh.

"Get real, Jack. We're in a police station, we don't have the skull, we've no way of getting it. We've got nothing. I've failed and we're going home."

Jack spun round. "It was there though, weren't it? It spoke to you, it wanted to be heard. Perhaps it couldn't find a way out, maybe it's trapped. We have to go back, you can't give up, not now."

Tom sneered at him. "Right, what d'you suggest? A magical escape from a locked room? If we do get out, we'd get caught. If you didn't know, Jack, we're in a police station. We can't drive, we don't know where we are…"

Jack threw his arms up in the air. "Listen to yourself. First sign of trouble, you give up. Just like school. Soon as you get something hard, you bunk off."

"That's not fair. This is nothing like that. This is massive, it's doing my head in but I've not bunked any of it."

"Because you haven't had a choice. You can't stop the visions. If you could, you'd have ditched 'em and never got on the plane."

"Like you'd do something different."

"Yeah, yeah I would. There's people depending on you. That Chief Satowa for one. You can't just walk away without a second try."

Tom glared at him. "Yeah, right."

Jack grabbed hold of Tom's shirt and slammed him against the wall.

"If you give up now, you'll let everyone down, including yourself. You've taken this quest, you can't just back out when a few hurdles spring up."

"A few hurdles…"

The door swung open. Jack relaxed his grip as they looked up.

"Dad!" they said in unison as they rushed over to them.

"Dad," Tom said, "I'm sorry about all of this, I didn't wanna leave like I did but I had to."

Jack continued. "You have to let us go though, we've gotta get on."

Tom's dad stood back, looking more stern than Tom had ever seen him.

"No one's going anywhere. Except back to Cornwall where you, my lad, are going to be sorry you started this escapade. The time and money we've spent looking for you. I had to get a loan out and take unpaid leave. We can't afford this, Tom. What the hell are you doing?"

Tom closed his eyes in despair. Don't let's fight, please. To add to his frustration, the booming voice and portly frame of Mr Griffith entered the room, closely followed by two policemen.

"No, leave me alone, I've every right to be here."

He shifted from one foot to another, eyes staring wildly. Tom looked at Jack in alarm – what's the matter with him? Tom's dad pushed him back.

"Piss off, Griffith. This is nothing to do with you and if you're not out of here in five seconds, I'll make you wish you hadn't been born. You've been a right pain the moment you've come over here. You ought to get yourself sectioned. If you're on holiday, then piss off and leave us alone. This is family business."

Tom stared hard, he'd never seen Dad so mad. Jack's dad stepped in.

"And I won't be responsible for what I'll do."

Griffith's face turned purple. "Don't start with me, boyo. Free country, I do as I want, the same as you."

Tom's dad formed a fist and punched him in the face. Griffith's nose cracked and blood ran down his chin. The police restrained them as Griffith fumbled for a tissue. Beads of sweat trickled down his forehead, he breathed laboriously and his fat fingers wiggled in frustration.

"I'll have you for that." His eyes narrowed. "I'll have all of you."

An authoritative voice shouted over the commotion. "Okay, that's enough! Any more and you'll be under arrest, every last one of you."

The room quietened as the owner of the voice strode into the room carrying Tom's rucksack. With three stripes on his sleeve, the sergeant had the physique of a bulldog and the severest of crew cuts. Slamming a folder down, he gestured for them to sit as he made himself comfortable behind the desk. The other policemen left the room.

Tom watched as the sergeant unzipped his rucksack.

"My name's Sergeant Tucker and I would like to know what you intended to do with this." He emptied the contents of Tom's rucksack onto the desk.

Tom gasped. There, among his belongings, was a crystal skull.

Jack leapt up. "Tom! You did it, it came to you."

Tom grabbed hold of the skull. "We're not finished. We can carry on."

The sergeant snatched the skull back and put it on his desk. Whatever Tucker was saying went unheard. Tom's eyes focussed on the skull. It must have got into his bag when he leaned against the wall.

"Atlantica, Atlantica."

Tom glanced around the room in desperation. We've got to get out.

The door swung open and Tom stared in horror. A man in a black suit and sunglasses entered the room, slammed the door shut and pointed his gun straight at Tom.

CHAPTER NINETEEN

"Give me the skull," he said.

Tom shivered. Everything about this man was ice cold.

The sergeant stood up slowly. "Okay, let's all take it easy here."

The gunman pulled out a wallet from his inside pocket and flipped it open. Inside was an ID.

"NSA. Give me the skull and no one gets hurt."

"Okay, buddy," said the sergeant, "you got it."

Tom glanced up. It's not the right place. It's not here, this isn't where he shoots. Think, Tom, think! As the sergeant came to the front of the desk, Tom grabbed the skull.

"No! You're not having it."

"Tom!" Dad went to grab him.

"Psh, psh. Run. Run," Zannor hissed, appearing suddenly through the far wall.

The gunman took aim. Tom struggled free of Dad as Griffith launched toward him. Tom pushed the skull into Zannor and a shot rang out. Zannor disappeared.

Tom stared in horror as Griffith slumped to the floor. Blood soaked quickly through his shirt and formed a pool on the lino. Jack threw up as their dads rushed to stem the flow. The door flew off its hinges as police charged in and aggressively wrestled the gunman to the floor. In the chaos, Tom grabbed his stuff and pushed Jack.

"Come on."

Running from the room, they sprinted down the corridor and went to jump the front desk. An officer dragged them back.

"Not so fast."

"Someone's been shot, there's a crazy man in there with a gun. He's threatening to kill everyone."

The officer let go, pulled a handgun from his jacket and raced toward the detention room. Tom and Jack leapt over the front desk and burst through the main door into the car park where Tom stopped dead.

"Mum!"

His instincts took over and he hugged her close. The first time that he'd done so for months. Jack tugged his sleeve.

"Tom, we have to go."

"No," Tom's mum said. "Where are you going? I know you wouldn't go without a reason. You tell me or so help me I'll drag you back in there."

Tom stood, amazed. Is she actually gonna listen to me?

"I'm on a quest. Don't ask what coz I'm not sure myself." His eyes pleaded with her. "You must trust me. When I know, I'll contact you. Promise. You have to trust me." He gripped her arm. "Speak to the Native Americans about the crystal skulls, they'll tell you. Please, you must believe me."

Tom looked into her eyes. They smiled back at him.

"Your dad'll go mad."

"Where's my mum?" Jack asked.

"Back at the motel with a headache," Tom's mum replied.

"You need to go in there," Tom said, "Mr Griffith's been shot."

"Oh my lord, your father!" She rushed towards the entrance.

"He's all right, Mum," Tom shouted, but Jack dragged him away.

"Come on, we have to get under cover."

They raced across the field to the copse where they sat, in silence, among the trees. Tom's head pounded as the shock of the shooting hit home.

"D'you think he's dead?"

Jack shook his head slowly. "Dunno."

"I've made his life a bloody misery and look what's happened."

"It weren't your fault."

"No? If I wasn't such an idiot at school, he wouldn't even be over here. If I'd have let that man have the skull, Griffith would still be here." He swallowed hard. "He threw himself in front of me, Jack, I saw him. He saved my life."

Jack closed his eyes and put his head back. He glanced across at Tom.

"You'd better make it a life worth saving then."

"How am I ever gonna do that? How can I do that if he's dead?"

They sat, slouched, in the long grass. Tom put his head in his hands. What am I doing here? Nothing makes sense anymore. He looked across at Jack, his clothes stained with sweat and dirt. Flopping his head back, he stared aimlessly through the branches.

"If you hadn't been with me back there, I would've given up."

"Well, I signed up to come with you."

"You're right about me, giving up. I didn't realise how easy I give in. Mentally, I mean. Just giving up on things at the first opportunity."

"Well, you've not given up on this, have you?" Jack said looking around. "Where are we, anyway?"

"Atlantica," Tom muttered.

"What?"

Whirring helicopter blades closed in. Jack slumped wearily.

"Oh Christ, we'll never outrun that."

Tom peered up incredulously. "No, wait." He pointed up. "Look!"

106

They couldn't mistake the Panama hat and sculptured moustache.

"DAVVERS!"

The boys ran to the hovering helicopter and dived in as Ed piloted the machine back into the sky. Chief Satowa and Davvers quickly buckled them into their seats. Tom looked down to see squad cars squealing after them. At the station, Tom's mum secretly waved. He held his hand up and smiled. Well done, Mum. He turned to Davvers and shouted over the noise of the engine.

"WHAT ARE YOU DOING HERE?"

"MANAGED TO GET ON A MERCHANT NAVY SHIP. GOT HERE QUICKER THAN I THOUGHT SO HEADED ON OVER. LOOKS LIKE YOU TWO HAD A CLOSE SHAVE."

"MR GRIFFITH'S BEEN SHOT. CAN WE FIND OUT IF HE'S OKAY?"

"YES, OF COURSE."

"WHERE ARE WE GOING?" Jack asked.

"WE'RE SWITCHING TO A PRIVATE JET AT SANTA FE, THEN ACROSS TO ROCKPORT ON THE EAST COAST. TINY PLACE IN NEW ENGLAND. YOU'LL LOVE IT. FROM THERE WE GET A BOAT OUT INTO THE ATLANTIC."

Chief Satowa leaned forward. Tom strained to hear his raspy voice.

"Our tribal people have given us their skulls. The time is near, the skulls are ready to speak. You must deliver them to your source and retrieve the thirteenth."

"ATLANTICA," Tom replied. "THE SKULL WHISPERED THE WORD ATLANTICA."

"Yes, my grandson. The skulls are becoming powerful. I sat with those we have been given and a vision came."

"ATLANTICA. WHAT DOES IT MEAN?" Tom said.

107

Davvers' eyes lit up. "IT MEANS EXACTLY WHAT IT SOUNDS LIKE. YOU'RE GOING TO THE OCEAN FLOOR."

Tom looked at him quizzically. What's he talking about? Satowa leaned forward.

"Many of our descendants follow a different path. They have returned to where they came. Where mankind cannot find them. To a place of myth and legend." His eyes smiled knowingly.

Tom stared at him. Descendents? Returned to where they came from? Ocean floor? Tom squeezed his eyes shut, forcing himself to think. Atlantica. Atlantica. Atlantic. Atlantic! He gawped, wide eyed, at Satowa.

"ATLANTIS!"

Satowa nodded knowingly as Tom grabbed Jack.

"JACK, THE LOST CITY OF ATLANTIS."

CHAPTER TWENTY

Tom had hoped to stop in Rockport longer. It reminded him of Cornwall, with its colourful sailing boats and fishing trawlers bobbing on the sparkling sea. He and Jack emerged from a shop in new jeans, trainers and cotton shirts. Slipping on his sunglasses, Tom stood back, posing.

"What d'you think?"

Jack grinned. "We look pretty damn good actually."

They walked to the harbour restaurant where they'd arranged to meet the others. Seated at a round table on a terrace overlooking the Atlantic, Tom ran his hands through his hair. It felt clean. Everything felt clean and so different to the hot, dusty desert. Freshly fried fish and chips arrived promptly and everyone tucked in enthusiastically. After a couple of minutes, Davvers sat back in his chair.

"Tom, old chap, I managed to get in touch with the hospital. Made out I'm a doctor. Your Mr Griffith is fine."

Hours of tension slipped away from Tom.

"The bullet went through him," Davvers continued, "missed his lungs and all his vitals. They patched him up and he's discharged himself. Apparently, he's on quite a few pills for depression. Lost his wife and son two years ago in an accident."

Tom pushed his plate away. Two years ago. He'd started at the school the same time. Tom hated the comprehensive and took it out on his new teacher. Griffith had been such an easy person to taunt. Now he knew why. He bit his lip. Christ, it's prob'ly me that tipped him over the edge.

"Can I have that?" Jack said, digging into Tom's leftovers.

Tom pushed the plate across and looked at Chief Satowa. "What's the NSA?"

Satowa, Ed and Davvers exchanged furtive glances.

"National Security Agency," Ed said, "they're part of our government."

Tom had stayed relatively quiet about the gunman but he opened up to the group and described everything in detail; how he'd shot Griffith and appeared in his dreams and visions.

"I'm even certain that he bumped into me at Heathrow."

"The NSA man is dangerous," Chief Satowa said. "They know about the skulls."

Tom sniggered. "But why would they be interested in ancient skulls. They're not a threat to the government." Tom sensed unease. "Are they?"

Ed put his fork down. "Our government will deny any links to myths and legends but the NSA know a lot of ancient prophecies are real because they spend time investigating 'em. If it's a threat to national security, they'll spend millions convincing people it's trash."

"But how can the skulls be a threat if they're saving mankind?"

"Because most of what they debunk can't be explained, it's not of this world, this civilisation. These things may be more powerful than the government. UFOs, psychics, Egyptian curses. They fear these things because they can't control them. And what they have no control over, they debunk or destroy."

"Grandson, the NSA man will try to stop you. This vision at a centre. What else did you see?"

Tom shook his head. "Nothing really, 'cept the hills at the back. They were really red. Like someone had covered them in rust."

Davvers slammed his hand on the table. "Of course! God, I can be so damned stupid. The Environment Gathering!" All

110

eyes focussed on him. "I put money in to finance it. It's in Sedona, Arizona."

Satowa nodded slowly. "Sedona – the hills are burnt red… very sacred place; this makes sense, this must be where the skulls are leading."

"Well, what are we doing here then," Tom said, "the thirteenth skull must be there."

"No, my grandson, the skull has spoken to you. Legend tells that one skull remains with its maker, the Atlanteans. We must visit and ask the keepers to release it."

"But it's a lost city," Jack said, "how're we gonna find it?"

Davvers carefully unfolded a piece of brown, stained parchment. Tom recognised it as a map of the world but it didn't look right. Some continents looked in proportion, others were missing altogether. Davvers noticed his expression.

"This map is thousands of years old. Here is Antarctica but, as you can see, there's no ice. Further along are some smaller islands that have long since disappeared. Across here is Europe before England became an island. Here's North America…"

"Well, that can't be," Tom said, "North America wasn't discovered until about fifteen hundred."

"Remember we're into the fourth age. Continents have been and gone since then. Between Europe and North America is this island here. It now lies at the bottom of the ocean."

Jack leaned forward. "What does this say – Atlantis?"

"We believe so, yes. We think the language is ancient Tibetan."

Chief Satowa nodded. "Many tongues and civilisations lie beneath the ocean and glaciers. The skulls are part of them."

"Clannah khall clanni sha. What does that mean?" Tom said.

Satowa smiled. "We believe 'we are all related' – that every part of the universe has a role to play."

Tom looked toward the sea. "Look, I've never been diving but I do know that even machines can only go down so far."

Chief Satowa raised his eyebrows. "You still doubt the skulls, my grandson."

Tom wished he had Satowa's confidence.

"How did Atlantis disappear?" Jack said. "It looks enormous on this map."

"They destroyed themselves," Davvers said.

Chief Satowa leaned forward. "Mother Earth became sick. Sick from the scars of war and pollution. She cleansed herself. Within one day and one night, earthquakes and floods were unleashed and the ocean swallowed Atlantis."

Tom shifted uncomfortably in his seat.

"It's happening again, isn't it?" he said. "The previous three ages all ended with natural disasters. Mother Earth can't cope with what we do. That's it, isn't it?"

Satowa brought out a long, clay pipe and began preparing it. "If the earth is not balanced, Mother Earth will fight to restore it. If she doesn't, many things will perish."

Tom swallowed hard. Ed slapped him on the back.

"Hey, dude, it's not all bad news. The skulls are gathering, they're giving us a chance to make it right."

Chief Satowa smiled. "Let us waste no more time. This gathering is in six days. It will take some days to retrieve the skull and make our way to Sedona." He stood up. "You must plan your visit to Atlantis."

That evening, Zannor hopped impatiently as Tom gave him the skulls belonging to the Hopi.

"Listen, where're you taking these? How am I gonna get them back?"

"Protect, I protect," Zannor screeched as he faded into the wallpaper.

At 3am, Tom woke in a sweat. The man in black broke into his dreams. But this time, he didn't just point the gun at Tom – he pulled the trigger.

CHAPTER TWENTY-ONE

Early the next morning, Tom sprawled out on a white leather sofa at the back of a luxury ocean cruiser. The sort that he'd seen on TV, anchored offshore at the Monaco grand prix. He zipped up his fleece and pulled the collar close. He'd learned the night before that the boat belonged to a French billionaire. Like Davvers, he'd had sight of the skulls and suddenly changed his life's priorities, deciding to finance environmental causes.

Chief Satowa stepped out to join him. He looked tired and weary from his travels. The boat lurched and pitched in the Atlantic swell and Tom helped him settle in a chair.

"Grandfather, why didn't you go to Sedona with Ed and Davvers? You look as if you could do with a rest."

"I will rest when I can be of no help."

Tom looked at a crew member as she passed by. "Do they know where we're heading? Most of 'em look younger than me."

Chief Satowa nodded. "Yes, my friend. There are many young people helping Mother Earth. It is a huge blessing – they have more sense than many elders."

"Were they chosen, like me?"

"Yes. Many young people have had sight of the skulls or an interest in the old ways. They know the power of Mother Earth and have chosen to return – to link again with nature." Chief Satowa heaved himself up. "It is nearly time. I must prepare." He wandered back to his cabin.

Tom sat back thoughtfully and watched the sun rise.

Cornwall seemed a lifetime away. He gazed across the swell of the ocean and smiled. Can't moan about being bored now.

But he slumped at the thought of Mr Griffith. It had become a dangerous game; people had been hurt, nearly killed. He tensed as another boat appeared on the horizon. Jack called out from the sitting room.

"Tom, Satowa's asked us to go to the front."

Tom pointed. "That boat's coming closer. It was on the horizon just a minute ago."

Jack dragged him away. "Prob'ly fishing. Come on."

They made their way to the bow and stripped off to their shorts and T-shirts. Rubbing his hands together from the cold, Tom caught his breath as Chief Satowa stepped on deck.

He'd changed from his normal cotton garb into a buckskin tunic and trousers, decorated in turquoise, red and yellow beading. His long grey hair had been tied into a ponytail and he held a wooden lance with a cloudy white glass fixed on the end. He stepped forward and stood between the boys.

"It is time."

A gunshot whizzed by Tom like a firework. The crew yelled and started the engines as the boat in the distance bore down on them. Uniformed police pointed rifles and an officer shouted at them through a megaphone.

"Cut your engines. Hands in the air. All of you."

When the engines cut, Satowa rested his hand on Tom's shoulder.

"Tom, Jack, you must trust me. There is a power and energy here – the skulls will keep you safe. Jump."

Tom, watching the gunmen, glanced at Jack, who had turned exceptionally pale. Satowa dived elegantly into the ocean and remained beneath the surface. Policemen ran up and down pointing their guns at the deep. An officer shouted across.

"We'll shoot anyone that tries to escape. Those are my orders."

Tom scanned the sea. Where's he gone? Jack sidled up to him.

"Flippin' heck, Tom. He's disappeared."

Tom watched the boat come alongside. It's now or never.

"Come on, Jack, what's the worst that can happen?"

And, as he dragged Jack overboard, he heard him yell, "DROWNING."

The cold sea took his breath and he instinctively swam to the surface where several bullets missed them by a whisker. Taking a deep breath, they dived under as more shots silently zoomed through the current. Tom led Jack underneath their boat and to the other side where they came up for air.

"Breathe normally," Tom said, through chattering teeth.

"I can't breathe, it's freezing."

Satowa sprang from the water, put his hands on their heads and pushed them under. Tom kicked and wrestled, fighting to hold his breath. His lungs burned as he struggled but Satowa kept him under. Finally, he gasped, preparing to give his body to the sea. But not a trickle of water passed his lips. He glanced, embarrassed, at Satowa.

Satowa still struggled with Jack, whose face had turned blue. Tom swam up behind and put his hands around Jack's stomach. Gripping his fingers together, he pulled in and forced Jack to breathe. His friend coughed and spluttered as air cascaded from his lungs. Jack turned angrily but Tom grinned broadly as his friend discovered the sea had no interest in taking him.

Above, the police boat moved around the cruiser. Satowa pulled them further down.

"We must go."

He swam down effortlessly, making his way through the ocean like an eel. Tom and Jack, now safe in the seas, imitated the dolphins as they swam by. A ball of herring scattered, alarmed at the sight of the strange human fish.

Tom saw plaice, monkfish and tuna. In the distance, whales lumbered lazily and sharks patrolled diligently beneath them.

The ocean spoke. Humpbacks bellowed their mournful cries, dolphins clicked, shoals of whiting flew by twittering in the current. A whole new world opened up; colossal underwater mountains and canyons, great swathes of seaweed and deep forests of kelp streamed hundreds of feet from the ocean floor.

Deeper into the murky depths, the sun refused to shine and daylight turned to night. Tom struggled to focus as the ocean turned black, silent and cold. All three joined hands.

Deeper and deeper, the great mass of ocean pressed down upon him. Tom had never experienced such a blackness. He whispered to Satowa.

"How much further? How do you know where to go?"

"Look down, you will see."

Tom saw nothing but darkness. He travelled blind, wondering how Satowa knew. Had he been here before? Satowa slowed down and came to a stop.

"There," he announced.

Tom stared down in frustration. There's nothing there…no wait! Yes, there, a twinkling light. And a sound. He recognised a solitary clang from a chapel bell as it tolled eerily through the depths.

Chief Satowa held up his lance and the clouded glass began to glow. Then, a piercing light emerged from the tip and shone down toward the ocean floor like a laser.

The chief waved the light slowly. "We wait – five rings."

Two. The sound of the bell tolled again.

Three. A melancholy sound.

Four. It reminded him of a time when the lifeboat crew had lost a man back home and the small chapel bell had tolled through the town.

Five.

"Come," Satowa said.

Beneath them, the sea began turning from inky black to turquoise blue, from the blackest night to the brightest day. Further down, Chief Satowa stopped and spread his arms out wide.

"My friends... Atlantis."

Tom gazed in awe as the sun shone on a magnificent island with sandy shores and rocky headlands. The tide lapped gently and a clear blue sky formed a canopy overhead.

"Amazing," he muttered.

Studying the island, it seemed to have a set structure. Hundreds of tiers, each layer made up of either forests, rivers, lakes or farms. Beautiful adobe homes blended into the scenery. People wandered about, smiling and waving to them.

He shook his head. Unbelievable. His gaze reached the top platforms, which resembled ancient Greece with their huge marble columns and steps.

Horses trotted up and down straight cobbled roads that led from the bottom to the very top.

"It looks like a gigantic 3D wagon wheel," Jack said.

Tom nodded, still trying to take it all in. In the distance he saw smaller, flatter islands with more farmland.

"Come," Chief Satowa said, swimming towards the top marble tier.

As they glided closer, Tom heard singing. He couldn't make out any real tune but it was hauntingly melodic. People up and down the tiers waved continually. Tom returned the gesture but couldn't make them out. In fact, if he looked straight at them, they seemed to disappear altogether.

Jack grabbed hold of his arm. "Tom, look at that!"

Rising in the distance was what looked like a cross between a hot air balloon and a cigar-shaped UFO. His grip tightened.

"Aeroplanes!"

Tom gawped at the flying objects as they hovered silently. The people inside waved frantically as the craft moved gracefully past them.

They arrived on the top tier, furnished with marble benches, tall vases of flowers and low-level tables. Above them, more flying machines floated by, slowing up to greet them, before moving on. Tom flushed. He felt like a celebrity at a film premiere, but waved politely at all the occupants. Jack leaned across and whispered.

"Tom, is it me, or do they keep disappearing?"

"Yes, I noticed that. If I look past 'em, I can see 'em really well but if I look straight at 'em, they're all transparent."

An elderly man, dressed in long, white robes, stepped onto the platform. Unlike everyone else, he didn't fade when Tom looked at him. He had kind blue eyes, a willing smile and a calmness radiated from him. He immediately made his way to Chief Satowa with outstretched arms. The two embraced and spoke quietly with each other.

Tom looked on, astounded. From that sort of welcome they must have known each other for ages. The man then came to Tom and spoke with a voice as smooth as honey.

"My name is Xavier. On behalf of the Atlantean people, I welcome you." He put his palms together and bowed. "Welcome, Tom Carver and Jack Newton."

Tom swallowed nervously and bowed.

"Please, come," Xavier said. "You are most likely needing refreshment after your journey."

He led them down some steps to a white marble terrace, onto which a map of the island had been engraved, then gestured for Tom and Jack to sit on the scattered silk cushions. A boy and girl placed bowls of fruit, bread and cheese down. They gazed sheepishly at Tom and Jack, giggled excitedly, then skipped away.

Tom and Jack tucked in straight away and savoured the warm, fresh bread and tangy cheese.

"This is fantastic," Tom said, "thank you so much."

Xavier bowed graciously. "It is our pleasure. These things you eat are grown and made here. If you are not too tired, Tom, and Jack, I would like to hear your story."

Jack couldn't take his eyes of the design on the floor. Xavier smiled and leaned forward.

"We will explain our island to you in good time."

Chief Satowa made himself comfortable in a hammock and quickly fell asleep. Tom, meanwhile, went through everything that had happened to him from the minute he'd found the first skull. Xavier listened patiently and flicked through Tom's journal, but appeared indifferent to the images taken on his phone.

"I have mixed emotions over material possessions."

Jack munched on an apple. "Why?"

His eyes softened. "It is time for us to speak with you. Of our story. It is also time for you to be re-acquainted with someone."

Tom cocked his head. "But we don't know anyone here?"

Xavier raised his eyebrows and walked to the edge of the platform. A much younger man joined him and he embraced Xavier before facing Tom.

He wore a rich chestnut-brown robe, and brown leather sandals with odd motifs stitched into them. His thick and wavy copper-brown hair shone in the sunlight, and his beard came neatly to a point. Long, slender, manicured fingers curled around a wooden flute. He stood happily as Tom scratched his head.

A bright blue dragonfly settled on the man's nose, his eyes crossed as he studied it. Tom laughed – the man chuckled. Coaxing the dragonfly onto his finger, he waved his hand and persuaded the dragonfly to flutter away.

120

"Psh."
Tom and Jack jumped.
"Zannor!!!"

CHAPTER TWENTY-TWO

After the welcome shock of seeing Zannor, Tom and Jack sat and relaxed with him on the cool marble terrace. He looked so different, so young and healthy, but Tom found it difficult to focus on him.

"Zannor, you look almost transparent," he said.

He'd never heard Zannor string a sentence together and his deep, melodic voice mesmerised him.

"The Atlanteans were formerly spirit. We took the form of flesh and developed bad ways. Our greed and wars were our undoing. Mother Earth ended our age. Here, in the ocean, we reverted to spirit and the old ways. We have no desire to return."

Xavier poured drinks for them.

"When you see Zannor in your world, he is agitated. It is hard to make the transition from spirit. It is many years since we stood on top of the earth, and shifting from ocean to soil takes its toll."

"I must apologise for not being with you at Mesa Verde," Zannor said. "Each journey to the atmosphere makes recovery longer. I was, unfortunately, still in Atlantis when you searched for the skull."

Xavier continued. "We sent prayers for the skull to find you."

Jack smiled. "Well, it worked. It just appeared in Tom's rucksack. We didn't even know it was there."

Tom touched Xavier on the arm. "You're not spirit."

"I am spirit but, for your visit, I have evolved to flesh. You can at least focus on me properly. Zannor remains tired from his journeys to the earth plane."

Tom shot a pleading glance to Zannor.

"Please, don't. Not for us. We can scc you, okay."

Zannor smiled gratefully. Xavier stood and bowed.

"I will leave you with Zannor. You will be given knowledge to help on your quest. Please, let us know if you require more refreshment. As spirit we have no need for food, but we continue to harvest. We have many visitors, especially now the skulls are gathering."

He bowed and left. Tom looked at the floor.

"Zannor, I know that's a map of the island, but why's it set out like this?"

"What do you think?"

Tom walked up and down the long spokes of the wheel.

"This wagon wheel shape. I think that different communities live in sections between the spokes."

Zannor raised an eyebrow in interest and looked at Jack. "And what do you think?"

Jack shook his head. "Well, when we came in, it looked like there were smaller structures down there. Are the poor people at the bottom and the rich people at the top?"

Zannor laughed quietly.

"What?"

Zannor held his hands up. "Please, do not take offence. It is wrong of me to laugh. It reminds me of Atlantean history. Let us walk. I have many things to show you. Please, follow me."

They followed Zannor down two levels and entered a wide, unending corridor. Tom looked both ways. To his left, the corridor appeared light and airy but, to his right, he saw nothing but darkness.

He looked left towards infinity. One wall had been decorated with a carpet that stretched into oblivion. There didn't seem to be any real pattern to it. Parts had become worn and faded, others looked vibrant in every shade and colour.

On the opposite wall, giant, wooden wheels rotated slowly and methodically. The continuous creaking and splitting of wood echoed ominously. Tom gazed in wonder; there must be thousands here, in all different sizes. Each wheel consisted of hundreds of spokes. It reminded him of the wheels you saw on old sports cars with smaller spokes coming off the larger ones. The wheel in front of him stood as tall as his house. Tom placed his hand on the ancient timber.

"What is this? Some sort of clock?"

"A good comparison," Zannor replied. "These were built by the ancients. The keepers of time and space. These are the circles of life. They have been turning since time began."

"Wow."

Tom studied the wheels as they progressed at a snail's pace. The wood was exceptionally dark with blackened knots and deep crevices.

"Each wheel represents a part of this planet's growth," Zannor said. "This one represents belief. The rim is the original belief, of the first people; it embraces the world and everything on it, animate and inanimate. But now, man has separated." Zannor pointed to the spokes. "They follow their own beliefs. Each spoke honours that but this creates unrest, wars. Mankind, unfortunately, does not honour the path of another."

Tom pointed to the circle in the middle.

"So what's that bit mean?"

"As with the outside, Tom, it is a circle – all beliefs are linked. All beliefs emerge from one, all beliefs lead to one. We are all one, we are all related."

Tom stood back, the wheels in his own head turning, digesting what had been said.

"So, our beliefs may follow different paths but, ultimately, they lead to the same end."

Zannor beamed and bowed his head graciously. "Come. This is the wheel that you should see."

Further down the corridor, Tom stopped in front of a much larger wheel with many more spokes, some of which had turned brittle and fallen away. Wispy ferns and green moss hugged the slowly turning structure. Zannor faced them.

"So, my friends, what do you think this represents?"

Jack looked at it quizzically. Tom caressed the outer circle.

"Look at all this vegetation." He looked at Zannor, hoping for some clues, but Zannor just nodded knowingly.

Tom's fingers gently followed the outline of the thick, damp spokes, careful not to damage what already appeared broken. His eyes lit up.

"I know! The rim is Mother Earth."

Zannor's smile beamed with enthusiasm. Tom looked back at the wheel.

"Each spoke is something that contributes to the balance of nature: animals, birds, people, forests – everything."

Zannor nodded, impressed. Tom pointed to the centre.

"They all live individually but come together here to keep the balance."

"Earth provides," Zannor said, "we give back what we take, to keep the wheel turning. Without one another, the balance of nature suffers. Clannah khall clanni sha. We are all related. I have more in common with an ant or a worm then another spirit."

Tom looked at him, confused. Zannor smiled.

"An ant or worm help to feed you. If they are not there to break up the soil, the food we sow would not grow. The rain would not reach the seeds to nourish them." He looked across at Tom. "Yes?"

Tom nodded thoughtfully. "Yes, I see what you mean."

"And providing everything's balanced," Jack said, "the wheel continues to turn."

Zannor stood between them. "And what do you notice about this wheel?"

"It's hardly movin'," Tom said, "this one's almost stopped."

Jack looked along the wall. "Maybe it's worn out. If it's been turning that long, it prob'ly needs replacing."

Tom spun round.

"That's why. That's why it's not turning much, it's worn out. The wheel is Mother Earth and the spokes are breaking because of what we're doing. We're taking everything and not giving back."

Zannor nodded. "This wheel has turned since the dawning of time. It is the original wheel. But this last millennium, as your world progresses, nature spirals out of control."

He pointed at different parts of the wheel.

"If you destroy the rain forests, this spoke will break. Droughts will prevail so this spoke will break. Wars have already damaged this section beyond repair. Pollution will break this spoke shortly. Animals in these areas suffer, so these spokes here will break." He turned to Tom and Jack. "What happens to the wheel?"

"It'll collapse," Tom said.

"If the wheel of Mother Earth breaks, she will want to cleanse herself before she is destroyed." He beckoned the boys away from the wall to get a better view of the corridor. "Observe. Many smaller wheels have already stopped. Each species on the planet has a wheel. Those that have stopped are extinct. They will not turn again."

Jack put his hands in his pockets. "And that's because of us. Humans."

"Only since man has walked the path of greed and technology. This path separates him from nature and many species on earth have vanished because of it. This wheel must repair. Man must restore the balance."

126

Tom wandered down the corridor. So many wheels had stopped. The wooden spokes were now brittle and rotten. Those that hadn't stopped looked close to doing so, but one caught his eye. Its young and shiny wood spun fast and furious.

"What's this one?"

"Ah," Zannor said, "this is the wheel of technology. It spins too fast. It will destroy itself if it continues."

"How?"

"Your technology progresses fast. It acts without caution. Medical and nuclear experiments; mankind meddles in technology it does not understand. This affects the earth. It should rotate more slowly. There is room for technology, but it must balance itself with nature."

Tom watched as the wheel whirled around. "If it carries on like this, it'll fall off the wall."

Zannor raised his eyebrows and nodded. Tom crossed to the other side of the corridor and caressed the intricate, soft, silk stitching of the carpet.

"How long is this corridor?" Jack asked.

"It would take several hundred thousand years to walk the length of it."

Tom and Jack stared at each other.

Tom looked up. "So, how high is it?"

"One hundred miles," Zannor said.

"But it'd stick out of the sea!" Tom said.

Zannor smiled. "We are in a different dimension."

"But what is it?" Tom studied the minute stitching as they walked along the corridor.

"This, Tom and Jack, is the tapestry of life. Every living being on the planet has a strand running through it. Each strand has several more linked through it. Trillions of beings making their way through life."

Tom stopped and studied one particular part. The threads

came to an abrupt halt; a tiny fraction of this carpet had been seriously frayed.

"What happened here?"

"The First World War. The scene of your vision. Many millions died. Not just men, but animals, birds and insects perished. And just along here? The end of the Mayan third age."

Jack stared closely at a chunk of bare carpet about an inch thick.

"We read about this. The end of the Third World was caused by floods."

Tom traced the worn carpet with his fingers. He could see through it easily but the occasional bits of stitching continued.

"Things still got through though, look. There're pieces of thread here, life carried on."

Zannor began walking back. "Come, let us have more refreshment."

Tom pointed toward the blackness. "What's down there?"

"That, Tom, is the future. We are not permitted to enter."

"But if the future's written, then we can see if we succeed."

"The future is only written once you decide your path. We do not write the future. You do. Come."

They returned to the terrace.

"Remember your own journey, Tom. You had a choice. To stay or go. Whatever happens, wherever you are, whatever you do, you have a choice. Once the choice is made, the tapestry weaves."

On the terrace, more refreshments had been provided and Tom, again, pointed to the design on the floor.

"Can you explain this now. What do the tiers mean?"

"Ah, yes," said Zannor, "they are not based on riches as you know them. On earth, riches appear to be measured in wealth, power, possessions."

Zannor pointed to Tom's heart.

"We measure riches by what is in here."

He tapped Jack's head.

"And here." He spread his arms wide. "These are tiers of knowledge."

Tom walked to the edge of the terrace and gazed down. Zannor stood behind him.

"We start at the bottom and work up. The elders on each tier teach philosophy, history, spirituality, art, music – all manner of things. As we progress through the tiers we gain wisdom and knowledge. No one person is richer or poorer than another, only in knowledge, but there is no ego because each helps the other."

"Then what happens? When you get to the top?" Tom said.

"Then our spirits progress. Some to other galaxies, some remain to share their wisdom." He looked at Tom, his eyes burning with intensity. "Others return to fulfil their destiny."

Tom stared back. Others return to fulfil their destiny? The intensity of Zannor's look hit him and his mouth went as dry as the Sahara. He looked across at Chief Satowa, who smiled knowingly.

"Are you telling me I'm a descendent...of Atlantis? From here?"

Zannor bowed graciously. "Yes. Part of your ancestors' souls are with you. Your soul has lived many lifetimes, often with the Navajo."

Chief Satowa joined them.

"Many people on the earth plane have ancestors here. They are helping Mother Earth. The young people on your boat are descendants. The plight for our earth is being heard but it is not enough to convince the men in power."

Satowa put a hand on Tom's shoulder. "Because they do not listen, the skulls are gathering. They will deliver their message."

"But if there's loads of descendents, why was I chosen? Why'd it pick me?"

Zannor poured him some juice. "You were the descendent who appeared as the skull revealed itself. It will choose someone with an old soul. The selected descendant becomes their spokesman. If any other tries to take the skulls, they are instantly killed."

Tom stood, unblinking. "That's why you'd only take the skull from me."

Zannor nodded as Tom carried on thinking.

"And Davvers was right about the legend, that a descendant would help gather the skulls."

Tom looked out over tier after tier of animals, farms, rivers, forests and fields. Everywhere, transparent spirits read, talked, laughed and sang. His ancestors had been a part of this. Jack playfully punched him.

"I always thought there was something strange about you," Jack said.

Tom smiled, then turned to Zannor. "So, what do I have to do to get the thirteenth skull?"

Xavier appeared on the terrace. "Nothing, my friend. It waits for you."

From within his body, a crystal skull emerged, which he placed on a small table. Tom knelt down, transfixed. The skull had a gold sheen surrounding it. Tom went to place his hands on it but Xavier stopped him.

"Do not touch the skull until you are ready to return. This has no vision. The world is not ready to accept all that it can share. You have what you need to succeed on your quest."

Xavier placed the skull on a small pedestal. "You must rest. Prepare for the gathering you are to attend. On the second morning, we will bid you farewell. Keep the skull in your vision, Tom Carver, let it inspire you."

***

On their last night, Tom leaned on a cushion and reached out to touch the skull, but it gently rebuffed him. Jack shuffled across.

"Tom, you should get some sleep."

"I will. I was wondering what's gonna happen at this meeting. How're we gonna get there? The police'll prob'ly be waiting for us at Rockport. S'pose we don't make it? I've got an awful feeling somethin' terrible's gonna 'appen."

"What d'you mean?"

"I don't know, I wish I did." He looked at Jack. "I hate to sound like a right nonce but you will stay with me, won't you?"

"'Course I will."

Jack laid back and stared at the stars. Tom eventually fell into a restless sleep, where he tossed and turned uncomfortably. His dreams took him to a large auditorium, where people stared at the ceiling in horror. The skulls bore down on him. The man in black pulled the trigger.

***

The following morning, Tom took a final look at Atlantis. Xavier and Zannor appeared on the terrace. Airships hovered silently alongside smaller flying machines, which buzzed them precariously. Thousands of Atlanteans had appeared to say goodbye.

Zannor transformed to flesh and he hugged Tom and Jack with great strength and love.

"I wish you well. We shall pray that mankind listens to the ancients."

"Will I see you again?" Tom asked.

131

Zannor smiled. "Not for some time. I have work here: to help with the wheels and teach those who come after you. I will visit." He touched Tom's head. "You will hear my thoughts. Meditate with Chief Satowa. If your mind transcends, we may communicate that way."

Xavier gave each of them a package, wrapped in cotton. "My friends. You will have little time to prepare. We are guilty of holding onto you for too long. A selfish, but enjoyable pleasure."

"Thank you," Tom said, taking his parcel. "How are we getting to Sedona? There's not much time."

Xavier waved the question aside.

"Tom Carver, descendant from the ancients, the skulls will do their best to guide and protect you. Be brave. That which they show, must be given."

Chief Satowa, looking relaxed and invigorated, hugged Xavier, promising to visit again soon, then stood by Tom.

The twelve skulls floated in line and the golden Atlantean skull hovered above. A blue electrical current crackled between them as they jostled closer. A blinding light flashed as the golden skull absorbed the others.

Xavier held the golden skull out for Tom.

"The skulls will reappear when they are needed. Good luck."

Tom swallowed hard, not relishing the long swim back.

"What if we're caught and we don't make it to Sedona?"

Xavier smiled knowingly and gestured for Tom to take the skull. With Jack and Satowa by him, he reached out and placed his hands on the skull.

And then he screamed.

CHAPTER TWENTY-THREE

Tom swore like his dad in a traffic jam.

He clung desperately to cold metal handles as the glass capsule he lay in shot through the bowels of the earth like a luge on a roller coaster. He could hear Jack screaming in the distance. His face turned to jelly as the G-force pinned him to the floor. A loud and constant whine whistled in his ears and the wind slammed and buffeted him aggressively.

His ears popped as the pod delved deeper. Above him, colours whizzed by in a blur. Earthy browns and greens changed rapidly; bronze to chestnut, jade to olive, sand to black; a montage of subterranean geology.

They rushed through a cavern of glittering minerals; diamond, opal and gypsum twinkled enticingly. Tom tried to move but his body felt like a ton weight.

The pod began to slow and Tom stole a glimpse of the sparkling caves. Turquoise, silver, nickel and gold flickered at him like stars in the Milky Way. He half expected to see the planets and moons of the solar system.

He accelerated and the G-force slammed Tom's head back as it zig-zagged, juddered, flipped and burrowed. He gripped tight, wincing as he sped recklessly, careering through the earth faster than a torpedo; the roaring gale screamed until his ears hurt.

When he thought he could take no more, the pod began to slow and brake. Tom shook his heavy limbs awake. The pod turned vertical, shot up, then came to a halt. Jack and Satowa stopped alongside and the lids above them opened.

Clutching his rucksack, with the skull safely hidden inside, Tom wearily threw his parcel out, climbed up the pod's indented steps and crawled onto a rocky hill. Jack and Satowa followed. The pods closed and immediately disappeared back into the earth. Tom stared incredulously. It's as if they'd never been there.

"Flippin' heck," said Jack, laying flat out. "I feel like I've been shot into space in a washing machine."

"Look like it, too," Tom said, looking at their torn shirts and shorts.

Unsurprisingly, Satowa looked calm and unflustered. Tom shook his head – how's he do it? There's more to him than he's letting on. He looked down the hill.

"Blimey, look! This is it, we're here."

Below him, hundreds of men and women made their way into a modern conference centre. Behind the building, majestic red rocks towered over luscious green trees that nestled against a deep azure sky. Sedona, Tom decided, looked like a really vibrant town with organic restaurants and open-air cafés.

"What's this?" Jack asked, pointing at the area where they had sprung from the pods.

Tom looked at a wide circle of small rocks.

"It's a wagon wheel!"

He walked around the circle, stepping from one rock to another, counting as he went.

"Twelve spokes. It's massive, looks like it's been 'ere ages."

"This is vortex. Very spiritual place," Chief Satowa said. "A place where Mother Earth is most healthy. Many minerals and magnetic fields are beneath this surface. Our people believe that our ancestor spirits come here for meditation."

"Hello, chaps, thought I saw you up here."

Tom looked up. "Davvers! Are we in time?"

"Absolutely, old bean, they're just going in. Lots of well known faces showing up. Come on, the sooner we get you inside, the better."

As they made their way down, Tom studied the activity beneath them. Police cars cruised by, security men whispered into walkie-talkies, bodyguards shadowed their charges, administrative staff buzzed about answering questions and ticking off checklists.

Tom stared at the diversity of people going in: African, Maori, Inuit, Aborigine, Asian, Tibetan; they looked stunningly colourful in their native costumes and chatted noisily between themselves. Alongside them, more conservative people entered wearing unadventurous dark blue suits. Davvers shouted for him to keep up.

Tom half ran and half slid down the hill until they reached the pavement across the road from the centre. He took a deep breath.

"I can't believe we've made it, Jack."

"Me neither. It all seems a bit surreal. Are you nervous?"

Tom shook his head confidently. "No, I'm not. I'm actually lookin' forward to it." The skull felt heavy in his rucksack and he glanced up at Davvers. "Because I know I'm doing the right thing."

Davvers didn't look at him, but he could see a smile beneath the moustache. Tom looked ahead, pulled his shoulders back and, imitating his military friend, announced, "Come along chaps. We've work to do."

Satowa raised an eyebrow, Davvers tutted and Jack chuckled, but as Tom looked up the pit of his stomach lurched. This isn't right. Unless the vision's wrong. A hand gripped his shoulder and yanked him around.

"Dad!"

Griffith hobbled painfully to a low wall, wincing as he sat down. Jack raced across to his parents but neither of them looked happy. Dad glared furiously.

"Don't think about talking your way out of this. You'll be lucky to see your next birthday."

Tom stepped closer but Dad held his hand up.

"You come near me, Tom, I swear I'll knock you from 'ere to kingdom come and when you get there I'll knock you back again. You've taken me and your mum through hell and back. You've lied, cheated, stolen, manipulated, your teacher was shot, for God's sake…"

"Darling?" Mum interrupted.

"Don't you stick up for him. Bloody quest. What d'you think this is, Superman? You're not living in a disaster film."

"Darling…"

"SHUT UP!"

Tom flinched.

Davvers stepped forward. "Now listen, old chap."

"Don't you start," Dad pointed his finger, "you're the cause of all this. Abducting kids! What are you, some sort of weirdo?"

"I say, that's a bit below the belt."

Tom clenched his fists. "ENOUGH!"

Davvers stepped back, but Dad glared angrily. Tom glared back.

"D'you think I did all this for fun? D'you think I wanted to cause you so much worry? D'you not think I would've told you what I was doing? If I thought you'd have given me a cat in hell's chance I would've told you."

Tom stepped forward.

"Why d'you think I left a note? I weren't just being polite, I wanted you to know I was OK. I didn't want this bloody quest, I didn't ask for it, I didn't wanna leave, I was torn apart walkin' out the way I did. I know I don't show it much but you and Mum are everything to me. I don't wanna hurt you."

His dad stared long and hard, scrutinising, psyching him out. He looked at Davvers and Satowa, searching for clues in their stance, their mannerisms. He watched the comings and goings of high profile delegates at the centre. Tom took a deep breath.

"I've got somethin' very important to do." He pointed at the conference centre. "In there. I've been chosen to do it. Just me. No one else. I can't explain it now but I'd rather have you in there with me than out here against."

He brushed past Dad and went to Mr Griffith. His teacher looked a shadow of his former self, hands shaking, his eyes watery and fearful. An empty man, a man on the brink. He'd lost everything and Tom couldn't help but feel responsible. He blinked back tears as he squatted down.

"Mr Griffith, I'm really sorry about what happened. About everything. I didn't know…about your family. I'm sorry. I'll make it up to you, I swear I'll make it up to you."

Mr Griffith managed an exhausted smile. Tom turned to his dad and held out his hand.

"You must trust me. For today, you must trust me."

Dad looked at his hand and across to Mum. After some hesitation, he reached out and took Tom's hand.

"Okay. But this'd better be worth all the aggro you've put us through."

Tom nodded as Davvers moved in.

"Listen, Mr Carver, I don't go around abducting–"

"I'm sorry," Tom's dad said, holding his hands up. "Obviously, there's more goin' on here than I understand."

Satowa broke his silence. "Your son is brave. A unique young man. In our old ways, he would be a fine warrior."

"I say, chaps, we really should be going in. The conference is due to start soon. Most people are inside."

Tom watched as their parents and Mr Griffith went into the centre. The streets had cleared and any remaining bodyguards did a final sweep before going in. He looked at his shoes and closed his eyes. This is it.

He looked up and a cold chill ran through him. Across the road stood the man in black, his gun pointing straight at Tom.

CHAPTER TWENTY-FOUR

Davvers put his arm across Tom and shouted to the man.

"There's four of us here, old man. You can't stop us all."

"I don't have to," he said. "My gun's pointing at the only one that matters. Tom Carver. You have the skulls. Either hand them over or I shoot you."

Tom stared at the gun. It can't end here. Not now.

"NSA," Satowa called out, "why do you want these things? They're nothing but myths."

"I'm just the messenger, old man. My orders are clear."

Tom swallowed what little saliva he had. "I'm not doing anything until you let these people go."

"No, Tom!" Davvers said, but Tom ignored him.

"Let these people into the centre. You can see they don't have the skulls. Search 'em if you like."

The gunman gestured for them to come.

"Go," Tom ordered. "Please. You must go."

Reluctantly, Davvers, Jack and Satowa made their way across. The gunman frisked each of them and ordered them into the building.

Tom stood alone.

"Okay kid. I've done what you asked. Now it's your turn. Give me the skulls."

"I don't have 'em. How can I have thirteen skulls here? All I've got is this rucksack and a parcel."

"You don't know the legend that well, do you?"

Tom's shoulders tensed. "What d'you mean?"

"The skulls are powerful with the chosen one. Without you, their message will either fail or won't be strong enough. You gotta have 'em somewhere."

Tom's jaw tightened. Shoot! How the hell am I gonna get out of this? Think, for God's sake, think. He closed his eyes.

A click broke the silence. The man had primed the gun.

Tom focussed on the skulls. Please, if you can hear me, I'm in danger, this man's gonna kill me, please, please help.

"Say goodbye, kid." Both hands held the gun. He took aim.

Tom opened his eyes, inspired. The gunman squeezed the trigger.

"WAIT!" Tom shouted. "The skulls are here. Have them." He tore his rucksack off and took out the golden skull. "It's here. All thirteen skulls are here, they were absorbed into this one."

The man in black placed the gun in his holster and wandered across to him. "See, kid, it ain't worth getting killed over some stupid legend."

He picked the skull up, then dropped to the floor writhing in agony. Tom sneered at him.

"You don't know the legend that well either, do you?"

The man's pained face stared up as Tom took the skull from him.

"It's only me that can touch 'em. The skulls will kill anyone who tries to take them."

Tom quickly turned, pleading with the skulls as he ran to the centre. Don't kill him, he's just doing a job, just keep him there 'til this is over.

***

In the centre's dressing room, Tom looked at himself in the mirror. He almost didn't recognise the weathered face and the longer dishevelled hair. Even his eyes held an aged wisdom about them.

He opened the parcel Xavier had given him and grinned. He'd convinced himself he'd been given a suit. But, in ten minutes, he'd changed into new jeans, a white collarless cotton shirt and a pair of leather sandals. They'd been worn before and the etching looked familiar. He smiled fondly. Of course, they're Zannor's.

The door opened and Tom glanced up.

"Ed!"

Ed gave him a bear hug. "You did it, dude, you did it."

Tom looked down. "Not on my own I didn't."

"You're here. That's what matters. We'll catch up later, but I wanted you to have these."

He handed Tom a turquoise bear pendant, attached to a leather strap. Tom turned it over in his hands.

"The bear represents wisdom, insight and protection."

As Tom secured it around his neck, Ed took out a suede bracelet and tied it around his wrist. He pointed at the images stitched on it.

"This is the falcon, it allows you to see clearly and act decisively. The wolf gives you courage to trust your instincts. The eagle gives strength and foresight. The buffalo represents survival. Finally…" Ed placed something in Tom's hand, "this is a fire opal. It's the stone of the idealist. We give it to those that seek the truth through their heart, not their head."

Tom took the round stone and held it up to the light. Flickers of amber, copper and orange reflected back at him.

"Thanks." He placed the stone in his pocket. Ed slapped him on the back.

"Okay, dude, I'm getting back to listen to the speakers. Davvers is gonna introduce you."

"Introduce me for what?"

141

But Ed had already gone. Tom's shoulders sagged. He wished he had some idea about what he would be doing. Another knock on the door and Tom gasped at his visitor.

Chief Satowa looked like he'd walked out of a history book. Resplendent in an eagle feather headdress, Tom gazed at the embroidered images of buffalo and eagles on his leather tunic and leggings. In his right hand, he held a wooden lance, decorated with beadwork, horsehair and feathers. A majestic eagle stood on his left hand, its eyes intense and alert. By his side, sat a sleek white wolf, his transparent eyes watched Tom knowingly.

"You look amazing," Tom mumbled.

"Special moments must be graced accordingly."

Satowa strolled in and Jack wandered in behind him. He'd obviously got similar clothes in his parcel and Ed had also regaled him in token jewellery. He handed Tom a tray with some turkey rolls and three coffees.

"Chief Satowa said we should eat."

Tom smirked. "Well, that suits you, don't it?"

Jack nodded happily as they sat down. Satowa perched the eagle on the back of his chair.

"Tom, I have been invited to sit on the stage. You must bring the skull to the stage and place it on the plinth in front of the microphones. Davvers will introduce you."

He stroked the eagle's breast.

"Take the eagle and wolf for strength and vision."

Tom sat forward. "Strength for what? I've not gotta give a speech, 'ave I?"

Satowa smiled and shook his head slowly.

"No, my grandson, I have no knowledge of what the skulls will do. But they are powerful, more powerful than speeches. You must be prepared."

Tom swallowed anxiously. Prepared for what? Satowa placed a hand on Tom's knee.

"Whatever they do, they will send their message through you. You must stay strong. With you, the chosen one, they will be at their most powerful."

Tom put his drink down. "What happens if I'm hurt or something, I mean if I get loads of visions, well…"

"Eagle and wolf will guide you. And Jack?" Jack looked up. "You must stay by Tom's side, be his strength."

Jack nodded, reaffirming everything. "Right. Okay. Stay by his side, be his strength. Right."

Tom heard a ripple of applause from the conference hall.

"My grandson. Close your eyes with me."

Tom did as Satowa asked. He spoke quietly.

"Great Spirit, protect Tom as he completes his quest. Help all two-legged understand the message given. Let them re-join the circle and rediscover the balance of nature."

Satowa transferred the eagle to Tom.

"Wow, he's heavy." Tom stroked its downy chestnut feathers, its eyes alert to the slightest movement. The wolf nuzzled his leg and, for a brief moment, he felt more animal than human.

Tom picked up the skull and they made their way down the darkened corridor and into the wings at the side of the stage.

Two minutes later, Davvers introduced Satowa. The chief walked out with Jack. Most tribal people stood and applauded enthusiastically. Satowa bowed graciously before sitting down.

Tom then heard Davvers begin talking about him. A wave of nausea swept over him. His foot tapped nervously and he shivered under the heat of the lights. Davvers raised his voice slightly.

"It is now time for me to introduce this extraordinary young man. Please welcome Tom Carver."

The wolf nudged Tom's jelly legs but they wouldn't budge.

He took a deep breath. Come on, get a grip. The eagle ruffled its feathers impatiently.

Tom bent down to the wolf. Its warm breath sent vibrations through his head. The animal's strength surged into his body and grabbed every fibre of his being. A newfound confidence welled, and standing tall, with his shoulders back, Tom strode onto the stage and acknowledged the applause.

CHAPTER TWENTY-FIVE

Tom placed the eagle and the skull on the podium. Looking out, he saw nothing but the glare of spotlights. He glanced over to the wings.

"Could you turn the house lights up please?"

Two heavy clunks and the auditorium came to life. Out of the hundreds of faces, the most important appeared to take up the front row. Tom swallowed apprehensively on seeing the US President and Britain's Prime Minister. A movement distracted him. He glanced across to see Mum waving proudly. He gave her a sheepish smile, then attached a small microphone to his shirt.

"I'm not entirely sure what's gonna happen or what I'm supposed to be doing. But I do know that I've had my own voyage of discovery on the way here. And it's a voyage that involves all of us."

The eagle jumped from its perch and flew around the auditorium, swooping low, almost touching the heads of the delegates. The tribal leaders marvelled at the bird, although the people in suits seemed annoyed that he'd brought animals with him.

"I've discovered that the choices we make could destroy us. Even individual decisions affect others."

He glanced across at Davvers, who winked back. Chief Satowa had his eyes shut but nodded slowly, and Jack gave an enthusiastic thumbs-up. Tom picked up the golden skull and held it high.

"Many of you put the legend of these skulls down to superstition." He placed it on a long plinth in front of him.

"I've discovered that the legend is real. That the words spoken by many of you today are meaningless. It's time for the ancients to speak, the Great Spirits that moulded this earth."

The US President smirked, raised his eyebrows and looked at his watch. Tom glared at him. A door opened at the back of the hall and four men in black suits came in. Tom stared at them in horror. A gentle hum emanated from the skull. He heard Satowa speak to Jack.

"My grandson, take your place by your friend." Jack stepped up quietly and stood by the wolf.

The hum increased in volume. The eagle soared up to the ceiling before swooping down and around the centre. The delegates' gaze followed its journey above them. A sprinkle of dust floated down. The eagle returned to Tom's side. The audience gasped as, one by one, twelve skulls emerged from the Atlantean skull and placed themselves in a line.

A delegate chuckled and called out, "Good trick."

Few laughed.

Tom noticed more dust and tiny fragments of rubble fall from the ceiling. The wolf edged closer to Tom, who instinctively fondled its ears. The men in black were closer now, feeling in their jackets for their guns.

A deep rumble vibrated around the hall. The delegates fidgeted as more rubble and dirt fell. Tom tried to stay calm, but he couldn't convince himself of anything.

Suddenly, huge fractures darted across the ceiling and un-nerving snaps and bangs shook every man and woman from their comfort. Delegates screamed as gigantic pieces of masonry fell and smashed into tiny fragments beside them. They scrambled, fighting to get to the exits.

But the exits slammed and locked.

The men in black took cover from the rubble thrown at them.

146

A small opening in the ceiling soon became a gaping hole. Tom stared in horror as the roof peeled back like a banana skin and revealed the darkening sky. Stars twinkled in anticipation.

His head buzzed – now what? He grabbed the wolf's fur and breathed deeply but nothing helped quell his fear.

"Come on," he mumbled, "for gods sake, whatever you're planning, let's get it over with."

Tom shrieked as he shot up through the roof, quickly followed by several hundred delegates. The jolt took his breath as he zoomed up into the sky. His limbs flailed wildly as he tried to balance; the eagle soared above and the wolf bounded alongside, unfazed by what had happened.

Tom looked back at the frightened delegates struggling beneath him. He saw very few tribal leaders, just people in suits.

As they soared further into the inky sky, Sedona became one of thousands of light clusters spread across the earth and nestled in dark blue oceans. To the east, the sun dawned on another day.

Up and up through the stratosphere, past satellites and docking stations. Jack struggled to stay with him.

"Flippin' heck, Tom, what's going on?"

They passed over the moon, deeper and deeper, through meteor showers, planets and distant moons, huge nebulas of purple and blue where celestial bodies glittered like diamonds.

Tom looked back fearfully. How far are we going? His desire to slow down prompted a buzzing in his head and he came to a halt in the middle of space.

The eagle circled majestically above and Jack and the wolf hovered close by. Tom stared in disbelief as he watched several hundred shocked delegates floating in space. Now what?

Silent. Windless. Odourless. Constellations shone clearer and brighter than he'd ever seen. Distant comets and meteors cruised on an endless journey through the cosmos. The dusty rings of Saturn floated effortlessly, her orbiting moons massive and empty. Far-off galaxies spun gracefully, silently.

The delegates stared through frightened eyes.

Tom whispered to Jack, "What do I do now?"

Jack pulled a face and shrugged.

An invisible force turned them all to face one direction. Tom saw movement in the distance. He squinted, trying to focus. Whatever it was, it was coming toward them. They looked like stars but they moved fast and darted about, almost dancing with one another.

As the lights closed in, each one the size of a house, he glanced at Jack in relief.

"I should have known," he said, as the thirteen skulls hovered before them.

The delegates flailed, horrified by the bobbing heads. The golden Atlantis skull spoke in a deep, hypnotic voice:

"Do not be disturbed. We mean you no harm. Before Tom Carver begins our journey, it is important for us to show that we exist. My age is five million of your years, I hold the knowledge of many and the wisdom of all. My resting place, Atlantis."

Tom observed the delegates. Some had relaxed a little, many floated, mesmerised. A few continued to lash out in fear. The skull resumed.

"In the beginning, the earth and all species lived as one. We existed only for knowledge and enlightenment. Now, man seeks only greed and power. He has detached himself from nature. This will be your undoing. Already we see the consequences: violence against man and nature. Your scientists play dangerous games."

The skull's power turned Tom to face the delegates.

"Tom Carver will lead our journey. He is descendant from those who made us. We become weak in our form. By joining with him, he will be our strength, our message will be strong. What you have destroyed cannot be undone. But another path awaits, should you choose it. Only you can decide, but ignore our warnings at your peril."

The skull pulled Jack toward them.

"Jack Newton, you will be shielded from what is to come. You must keep your strength."

Jack gulped and nodded. The skulls gathered around Tom.

"Tom Carver, we must return to spirit. We ask your permission to join with your mind."

Tom glanced anxiously across at Jack, then back at the skulls.

"Okay."

The skulls began to shine brightly as they fused into one glowing ball and slowly reduced to the size of a pinhead. Tom jumped as a beam of light shot into him like a blowtorch. He felt a dull ache behind his eyes that vanished almost immediately. Jack stared at him.

"You all right?"

Tom moved his eyes – up, down, left, right – and then nodded.

"I think so."

His head buzzed. He looked across at the stunned delegates. Jack whispered to him, "What now?"

Tom scanned the universe and spotted a blue dot hanging in space. As he pointed he noticed the delegates had turned with him. He grinned in realisation – where he turned, the delegates turned. His head buzzed and thoughts rattled by like ticker-tape.

"That tiny blue dot is our home. Everything we have is there. Everything that's ever happened has happened there. Mother Earth."

He floated around the group of formally-suited men and women.

"She's our home, our only home. She feeds us, nourishes and shelters us. We have nowhere else. It's not a piece of rock – it's a living planet. She feels, she breathes, the same as you and me."

The eagle began flying towards earth and the wolf nudged the back of Tom's leg.

"We've separated from her. She's the one person that provides everything to keep us alive and we've forgotten her. If she's destroyed, we're destroyed."

Tom and Jack shot forward and accelerated at an impossible speed. Nebulas, planets, moons and constellations became one long blur as billions of miles vanished in seconds.

Closer to earth, Tom slowed down and hovered above the stratosphere. The shocked delegates floated alongside, struggling to breathe. Tom shouted across to them.

"You're seeing the earth as it was thousands of years ago."

The skulls pulled them into the atmosphere. The rich Atlantean voice whispered to Tom, "Take them, lead them, show them, remember your visions, follow your heart and feelings. We will guide you."

Tom's eyes opened wide with anticipation and, followed by his startled entourage, he plummeted down to earth.

CHAPTER TWENTY-SIX

The great eagle spiralled down. Tom and Jack copied his flight, stretching their arms wide, pretending they too had the same feathered wingspan.

Tom shouted across to Jack, "Isn't this fantastic?"

Jack glanced back. "Look at them."

Tom chuckled as the delegates stumbled behind. The warm thermals took him higher and as he crested above the clouds, he turned and swooped back down to rejoin the group. The continent below beckoned. His head buzzed, he knew exactly where to head for.

"The rain forest!" he announced excitedly as they landed clumsily on top of the trees.

The eagle perched itself on the tallest branch. Tom, Jack and the wolf landed alongside.

"Strange fruit," Jack said, pointing at the hundreds of delegates perched precariously across the canopy of green, their suits already dusty and misshapen.

Tom gazed up at the cloudless sky. The delegates followed his gaze. If the skulls wanted them to see something, they copied him. He rolled his eyes – and we think we're advanced. Thousands of tiny, twittering, black birds swarmed around to greet them before disappearing among the leaves.

The wolf glided down into the foliage and Tom and his entourage sunk beneath the canopy. A wall of humidity covered him in sweat. The thickness of the trees refused the sun entry but, as Tom hovered above the forest floor, the ground misted up like a steam room.

A cacophony of sound bombarded his senses.

"Listen to this," he shouted, "the sound of nature! This is a city. A city of animals with everything they need to live."

He floated through the trees and pointed at whatever he could see. The delegates 'ooed' and 'aaahhhdd' with every encounter.

Howler monkeys leapt from tree to tree whooping at one another with ear piercing screeches, their babies munching on sopping wet leaves; bright yellow birds of paradise squawked noisily, their black and turquoise plumage vibrant in the green; hundreds of birds in unimaginable colours darted around him, as red as a fire engine, as yellow as the sun, as green as the purest jade. Translucent azure blue butterflies fluttered cautiously; cute furry bats feasted on fruit trees; muscular jaguars monitored them warily; a whoosh of hummingbirds sped by, and bright red knobbed hornbills fed on whole figs. Plump hoatzin birds with orange mohicans chomped loudly on vegetation.

Jack called over to Tom, "This is bloody amazing."

Tom grinned. The delegates behind nodded in disbelief and stared in awe at the array of life and colour.

Climbers and ferns wrapped themselves around the trees. White orchids bloomed and mushrooms the size of dinner plates sprouted from their trunks. Mauve vine flowers as big as basketballs bloomed across the forest. Passing birds pinched nectar from red mistletoe.

Tom held on tight as he sat on a branch and watched as the delegates began to relax. They'd been bowled over at the diversity of life, the crescendo of sound, but they'd remained close to Tom. Now, they ventured out further, touching the trees, studying the birds and stroking the velvet petals of rare plants.

"The lungs of the earth," Tom shouted. "Without this, we wouldn't survive."

Above the chattering of animals, insects and birds, he heard the call of the eagle. The wolf, taking water from the dripping leaves, glanced up and began running along an invisible path to the sky.

Jack gasped as a forty-foot long anaconda snake eased its way slowly along the forest floor – its body the width of a football. Tom stared apprehensively as it glided silently through the undergrowth. He looked across at Jack.

"Time to go I think."

The eagle called again. Tom shot up, out of the oppressive heat, into dryer, fresher air. The delegates popped up behind him.

He winced. His muscles tensed. The familiar searing pain from his visions returned, but this time, Tom heard the delegates scream in agony. Only Jack remained immune. He rushed over to Tom.

"What is it? What's happening?"

Tom pointed. Everyone turned.

The rain forest began disappearing. Hacked down by axes and great lumbering machines. The luscious green canopy plummeted to the floor. The smell of dead vegetation and petrol fumes filled the air. Terrified birds flew helplessly and animals screeched and ran blindly through the trees; thousands lay dead and injured. The forest that had stood for a thousand years fell like autumn leaves.

Jack grabbed Tom. "What're they doing?

"Carting it away," Tom said breathlessly. "Clearing for crops. For us to make into things we don't need. Look at the plants."

The once perfect orchids wilted as the sun scorched the life from them. Monkeys and jaguars, driven from their homes, scrapped for food. The incessant whirring of the chainsaws came closer. The forest fell beneath them, never to rise again.

As each tree fell, Tom flinched and screamed. Blood began to seep from cuts and gouges in his arms and legs and he gasped for air. The delegates suffered the same fate and cried out for help. Tom leaned on Jack for support as he struggled to shout across to them.

"You're seeing earth as it is now. You're feeling what she feels. Her lungs are being ripped out. These animals have lost their home." He pointed to a family of howler monkeys. "They're completely lost, don't know what to do."

"Can we help them?" a woman said.

Tom shook his head.

"Nothing can be done. This has already happened," Tom said as the delegates looked on helplessly. The family that had played together now huddled in fear.

Tom's head buzzed as they were catapulted across the globe like an arrow from a crossbow, their wounds slowly healing as they went.

They hovered above a turquoise ocean. With a glance at Jack, Tom grabbed his friend and plunged under. Before the delegates could catch their breath, an invisible force pushed them beneath the ocean. Tom and Jack drifted effortlessly at the bottom.

"Don't be alarmed," Tom reassured the gasping delegates. "The skulls will protect you – you can breathe here, you're safe."

He and Jack floated calmly as the delegates' terror turned to wonder and astonishment. The warm, crystal-clear water caressed them gently in the current.

"Come on." Tom led them to the shallows. "You've gotta meet the families who live here. Millions of 'em work together to help the oceans stay alive."

He led them to an enchanted paradise heaving with fish – yellow and black, transparent glass, blood red, electric blue and mustard – all swimming madly through the riotous orange coral. A host of banana-yellow sea horses cantered by on the waves feeding on plankton that floated up from the ocean bed. Millions of fish – ducking, diving, bobbing, weaving – constantly moving.

The delegates swam closer. Tom smirked; they looked so weird down here in the ocean. He swam across to them.

"This reef started forming four million years ago. It's the most complex eco-system in the sea. The fish help each other evolve; they work and provide for one other. That helps our food chain too and our oxygen."

He swam beyond the reef to the deep blue depths, beckoning his companions to follow. Jack swam alongside him.

"This is excellent. Have you seen the look on their faces?"

"Yeah, and take a look at this."

In the stillness, Tom and the delegates waited.

"Listen."

A mournful cry echoed through the deep, followed by another, then another. It sounded sad and forlorn but Tom smiled.

"We're not the only ones who like a chat," he told the delegates. "This lot like a chat, and like all mums, they're telling each other how special their kids are."

From the distant blue, a herd of humpback whales eased by, their tiny calves sheltering beneath their mums.

"My goodness," a delegate said, "there must be hundreds. Where're they going?"

"Up to the Arctic. Three thousand miles. When the seasons change, they move to where there's plankton, and that's the Arctic."

The whales glided close by, allowing everyone to touch and stroke their huge white underbellies. The sonic clicks and sighs increased as they circled around to enjoy the company of the odd fish in dark suits.

Tom stood on the ocean floor with the wolf and Jack.

"Look at them, they're like different people."

The delegates laughed and played like children among the gentle giants. Tom closed his eyes and sent thoughts to the skulls. Show them more, let them see more.

Seals began darting in and out and turtles swam by to give rides to the men and women who had now freed themselves of all restraints. Tom's head buzzed. He looked up in wonder.

"My God," he mumbled.

Everyone watched in awe.

Quietly descending and drifting by with the grace of a ballet dancer, five immense blue whales breezed by, almost knowing they were the encore of a very special show. The delegates swam to meet them, looking like tiny bowling pins against the kings of the sea. Tom swam up to the whales – he'd never experienced anything so gigantic, and yet so gentle.

The wolf nudged him. Although deep under the ocean, Tom could see the shadow of the eagle through the rippling water above.

His stomach flipped as the pain shot through him. He doubled up as Jack rushed to his side. The delegates scrunched in unison, pleading for some relief.

"Blimey," Jack said, "look!"

The vibrant purple reef turned bleached white.

Tom's complexion matched the coral; a nausea spread through him as he became cold and clammy. He sunk to the floor and put his head in his hands. Jack stared and grimaced.

"Christ, you look awful."

Tom faced the delegates. "Poisoning. That's what this is. Four million years gone in a few decades. Destroyed by mankind. It's not doing it yet, but this will affect our food chain and the levels of carbon dioxide in the air."

The delegates looked visibly shaken as the thriving community dwindled before their eyes. Plankton disappeared, the fish vanished and the reef hugged the seabed like a phantom.

Tom's head throbbed; he scratched at a rash that rushed across his skin. Some delegates had vomited, others held their aching heads and all of them had swollen blotches appearing on their hands and face. Tom so wanted to lie down but the skulls urged him on. Tell them, tell them.

"This reef's off the coast of Africa. You saw it as it was about six hundred years ago, but this is what it's like now. All life has gone, and if you look behind you there's not much there either."

They turned to where they'd played with the whales, a near lifeless ocean. A delegate turned to him.

"Where are the blue whales?"

"You won't see any," Tom replied. "They're nearly extinct. Haven't been back this way for years."

The group said nothing. Tom's energy dipped further. Don't stop, he muttered, keep going. His head buzzed as he focussed again.

Speeding out of the ocean like a cruise missile, they surfed the jet stream, through misty clouds and black storms to a land of lush green pastures, clear rivers and mountains. Having regained some of his energy, Tom posed like Superman alongside the eagle. They flew up a sheer rock face then hurtled down a cascading waterfall and into the icy waters of a raging river. He found himself leaping in and out, mimicking the salmon alongside. The delegates whooped as they skimmed above the waters with him.

Finally, Tom came to a halt and stood in the shallows.

Millions of salmon swam against the current, through crevices and small water torrents to reach their birthplace. Purple plants and heathers hugged the riverbank. Tom, Jack and the delegates stood among the heaving mass of salmon. They picked individual fish out and threw them upstream, helping them on their way.

Eagles and gulls swooped down to grab an easy dinner. Brown grizzly bears strolled into the shallows and, with a flick of their huge paws, plucked gasping salmon out onto the grass for their delighted cubs.

Tom floated up, spread his arms wide and hovered above his entourage.

"Nine hundred miles they've come. Three million salmon." He led them on to the spawning ground. "They 'ave their kids here. Once they're born, the adults die." He pointed to the river's edge. "Their bodies feed the riverbank for other animals and plants."

The delegates hung on Tom's every word. Tom remembered what Zannor had said.

"It's a circle. You destroy one thing, it sets off a chain. You end up destroying something else."

The stabbing pain flashed quickly this time. The bubbling river gradually slowed and became a shallow stream. Where millions of fish had been, just a few hundred made their way upstream.

Tom chewed his lip and fought back his tears. The eagles had gone, the bears never appeared and the plants that had grown so plentiful on the water's edge had died long ago.

An overwhelming sense of sadness draped over him. It wrapped up all that was good and took it away, leaving him lost and desolate, as if everything closest to him had passed on. The delegates wept and comforted one another.

"The earth is sad," Tom said. "She wants us to know how she feels. So many lives have been affected here."

His head buzzed. The wolf nudged him. The eagle called. The skulls pulled them up to the skies.

"Clanni khall clanni sha," they whispered. *"You must be strong, Tom Carver, you must be strong."*

A surge of adrenalin rushed through him as the skulls

pulled them aggressively. The wolf sensed his anxiety and nuzzled closer. He glanced back at his friend.

"Jack, stay with me, mate; I think things are about to get worse."

CHAPTER TWENTY-SEVEN

They crested the highest peaks of Snowdonia, explored the deep gorges of the Grand Canyon, skimmed the trees of the Black Forest and shivered in the cold beauty of Everest. Alaskan glaciers creaked ominously beneath them, and snapping crocodiles rose from the bubbling Amazon. They dived over Niagara Falls and braved stinging burns as gales whipped up the Sahara sands.

But as the wonderful sights increased, so the hurt and suffering intensified.

With every twist and turn, invisible forces slammed into them like a demolition ball. Their bodies became lolling rag dolls, winded and floppy. The delegates begged for a rest but the anguish continued relentlessly. Jack, protected from the forces, held Tom tight.

Over the once lush hills of China, Tom choked on putrid fumes from a thousand coal mines. He retched and coughed up filthy black saliva as soot sucked the air from his lungs.

In a flash, the forests of Russia transformed into smoky industrial cities, their chimneys spewing dense clouds of gas and carbon into the atmosphere. Tom balked and heaved on the sulphurous fumes.

He stared at the shattered delegates. Their clothes hung loose and their eyes had sunk deep into their sockets.

Fierce lightening fizzed around and the group sped across to ancient temples and gardens. Jack grabbed hold of him.

"Tom! These are Mayan temples. I saw these on the Internet at school."

They hovered above vast flat-topped stone pyramids, but in a flash they'd vanished. The delegates screamed and Tom groaned and collapsed onto Jack.

In their place, a monumental refuse tip. Above, gulls fought one another, scrapping over rotten food and decaying animals. Tom gagged on the stale air and scrambled to get away from the dirt and stench. His legs buckled.

"OW!" Tom bent down, the pain dug deep inside him. The delegates pleaded for respite but on they travelled.

The deep blue Aral Sea sparkled enticingly in Kazakhstan but, in the blink of an eye, the colourful fishing boats lay marooned in the sand. Jack gaped at the dry ocean floor.

"Where's the sea gone?"

Tom clung to him and whispered hoarsely, "River, diverted."

The disappearing sea sucked him dry. Every ounce of life ebbed away. Jack held onto him helplessly.

The buzzing in his head intensified.

Every car-crammed metropolis suffocated him; every glacier crashing into the ocean drained him; every forest turned to concrete forced the air from his lungs; every blast, cut and drill kicked and thumped them all into oblivion.

Tom slumped. Even his skin hurt. He tasted blood and breathed laboriously. His eyes felt gritty and sore. Every muscle screamed and burned like a hot poker. The slightest noise exploded in his head like a bomb. He checked on the delegates. They couldn't take much more, especially the older ones. Jack propped him up.

"Tom," Jack said, "you've gotta stop, you're gonna kill yourself."

Tom shook his head, struggling to stay conscious. "No, we have to go on. We stop when the skulls tell us."

He could see Jack's concern but he couldn't stop now. The delegates looked dead on their feet but that wasn't enough. He looked at Jack.

161

"There's got to be something more, Jack. This is still the present, this is what's happening now."

The wolf barked and licked his face. He didn't know how but the wolf's breath seemed to give him some strength. Above him, the eagle called.

The skulls pulled; his head buzzed and spun furiously.

"Clannah khall clanni sha."

His eyelids drooped, every movement took the very essence of life from him.

"Tom, stop, please," Jack pleaded.

He drifted in and out of consciousness. Jack shook him hard.

"Let's go back. They've seen it now. Look at their faces; they've got the message, I'm sure of it. Come on."

"Please," Tom muttered to the skulls, "you have to slow down. I can't go on."

Jack shook him again. "Tom, tell them to stop."

Suddenly, they shot up into the cosmos with a force that contorted their bodies in ways he didn't think possible. Tom sighed heavily as he hung suspended in space. Through his bleary vision, he saw the delegates hanging like meat on hooks.

"This isn't finished," he said as some of the delegates raised their objections. "You're feeling the earth now, but we need to see the future. You need to see what's gonna happen if we carry on the way we're doing." He turned to Jack. "They need to see how angry she'll be."

Jack looked at him in desperation. "But you won't make it."

Tom forced a smile. "It's my destiny, Jack. I have to do it. I'm not bunking off this one."

Jack looked beside himself. "You keep hold of me. Whatever happens now, we keep hold of each other."

162

Tom nodded sleepily. The eagle called. The wolf licked his ear and he turned and gazed down at a very troubled-looking earth.

CHAPTER TWENTY-EIGHT

Tom didn't know what to make of it. A mass of thick swirling cloud covered the planet. The pictures he'd seen from space always showed great swathes of blue but he couldn't see any. He hovered anxiously and looked at Jack.

"What d'you think?"

Jack shook his head. "Dunno."

"Only one way to find out."

With Jack and the wolf alongside him, Tom slowly made his way down. He eased through the stratosphere, into iron-grey skies, where the view before him went beyond comprehension.

The huge swirling mass revolved in a monstrous spiral. Heavy, dense storm clouds laboured, gradually building momentum. They bubbled and jostled, their evil blackness sucking them in. Jack pulled him back.

"Look!"

A knot tightened in Tom's stomach. In the centre of this hideous mass he saw a spectacular circle of clear air.

"Bloody hell," he said, "a hurricane!"

He stared, open-mouthed. It covered half of North America. He edged up, away from the roar. The delegates watched him anxiously.

"Right. We're going in," Tom announced.

Against the deep rumbling of the storm, he heard the delegates shouting and pleading. He almost felt sorry for them. Jack fidgeted beside him.

"I'm not going down 'til we're secure." He looped the

leather belt from his jeans through Tom's and fastened it tightly. "Where you go, I go."

With a determined look, they gently descended, but the maelstrom quickly snatched them in.

Booming thunder crashed as violent gusts catapulted them around the swirling vortex. Round and round, faster and faster, spinning, tumbling, turning through cold, blinding, torrential rains. The storm roared angrily as he dived further to escape the torrent.

"HEAD TOWARD THE EYE," Jack shouted.

Tom dipped beneath the clouds, but the momentum of storm sucked them back. He stared in horror as delegates collided with each other and disappeared into the murky mists. Tom grabbed the wolf's fur and forced them forward and into the ominous calm of the eye.

He floated; his thumping heart almost leapt from his chest. The dark, billowing clouds circled him, threatening to pull him back. One by one, the delegates tumbled into the calm with the look of hunted animals.

"My God," Tom mumbled as he looked down upon an obliterated land.

Splintered wood and concrete boulders were strewn across flooded plains and valleys. Muddy water cascaded through land where homes and offices had stood. People, pets and livestock fought in vain as the torrent washed them away. Those still alive clung precariously to the tops of trees and fallen roofs. Rescue helicopters careered out of control as fierce crosswinds sent them crashing to the ground in flames.

The hurricane spiralled closer. Tom felt the raging winds tug them in, hurling them around like a spin drier. The driving rain forced his eyes shut, the hurricane took his breath, and he sent up a silent prayer: don't let me die.

The storm spat them out into daylight, where they tumbled from the sky.

"LOOK OUT," Jack yelled.

They hit the dirt like a sack of bricks.

"Oooohh, Christ." Tom doubled up, feeling his foot. It had already begun to swell.

Jack ripped his shirt off. "Here."

He wrapped it tightly around Tom's ankle and tied it in a crude knot. "How's that."

Tom winced but nodded gratefully. "Thanks."

He looked around. They'd all landed awkwardly but the delegates, at least, had survived. They helped one other, tending broken bones, sprains and cuts.

"This is Los Angeles," Jack said. "There's the Hollywood sign."

Tom manoeuvred and looked at a sprawling city that seemed to consist of buildings and motorways. The air felt heavy and the dirt in his hands fell to dust. He turned quickly.

"I've been here before! When I found the skull on the beach. This is where it took me – my first vision. The ground broke up, there was a girl…" He searched for her but she didn't appear.

A band of filthy yellow smog hovered over the city. Cars and lorries shunted slowly, horns blasted impatiently. Beneath him, the earth rumbled.

"Hold tight," Tom announced. "This is a rough ride."

A thunderous roar and the whole ridge divided as land fell away in front of him. Tom stayed close to the ground as the hill to one side dissolved to liquid. Huge mounds of earth cascaded in waves, carving through streets and uprooting whole communities, folding them into the earth like cake mixture.

Flyovers collapsed, trains and cars careered off bridges, explosions popped randomly as cables and gas mains ruptured. The broken earth swept the city toward the sea. Thick dust turned the sky brown. Tom screamed at the shaking delegates.

"GET LOW TO THE GROUND!" He pulled at Jack. "Try not to breathe it. You'll choke to death."

He could only imagine what was going on in the valley. He heard crashes, screeching, screaming, shattering booms and metal being twisted and torn. It sounded like the end of the earth. The delegates coughed violently as the dust cloud blew over them.

The rumbling stopped and, after a few minutes, Tom ventured to the edge of a newly formed cliff. As the dust settled, he saw shadows: blurred images of broken structures and crumbled concrete. The silence seemed eerie, ominous. Too ominous.

"Listen," Jack said.

Tom heard it: a new sound; the sound of water.

He watched, powerless, as a new coastline formed over the once thriving metropolis. The ocean raced down shattered streets, drinking up every available space. Within minutes new rivers and lakes had formed. The debris of an entire city floated like driftwood and the cries of its residents carried on the breeze.

Tom clasped his hands to his head and curled up in a ball.

"AAAAAHHHH!"

Jack held him. "Bloody hell, Tom, what's wrong?"

Tom's muscles went into a torturous spasm. He gripped Jack's arm.

"Something's ripping my insides out."

The wolf barked anxiously, pawing and nudging. Jack stared uneasily at the devastation around him.

"We've gotta stop. Look at you, look at the delegates. Someone's gonna get killed."

"No!" Tom said, coughing. "We have to keep going."

"You're spitting out blood." Jack looked up to the skies. "IF YOU CAN HEAR ME, TOM'S INJURED, WE'VE GOTTA COME BACK. YOU MUST STOP THIS."

"NO JACK." Tom clamped his hand over Jack's mouth. "We're not finished." He winced. "I'll be all right."

His head buzzed. The skulls snatched them up, and within seconds, had placed them on a small island beach in the Pacific.

Jack laughed nervously. "Are they giving us a rest?"

Tom welcomed the lapping turquoise seas. The sun warmed the light, powdery sand and palm trees rustled lazily in the breeze. Behind him, he saw a small community of people in straw huts. He heaved a big sigh, untied himself from Jack and flopped back.

"I'm starving," Jack said. "They must be too."

The delegates nodded wearily.

"There must be food in the village," Tom said. "Let's just rest for two minutes."

The eagle screeched at him and headed inland. Tom sprang up nervously. The trees shook as thousands of birds took to the skies. Animals scurried from the beach. The wolf nudged Tom violently, barking as if his life depended on it.

"What? What's the matter?"

Jack watched closely. "Tom, why're they all leaving?"

Tom frowned. "I dunno, there's nothing happening, what're they frightened of?"

A delegate shouted out, "Something's happened to the sea."

Tom looked. The sea's not right. It's been drawn back. Too far back. Small fish floundered, crabs buried themselves hurriedly.

He spun round. "GET OFF THE BEACH! GET OFF THE BEACH! RUN!"

Tom flinched in pain with every step. Through the village, they made for the hills as the residents looked on, confused.

The eagle called and the wolf stopped. Tom stopped and stared.

"What? What is it?"

The wolf pawed a tree. Realisation dawned.

"GET UP. CLIMB THE TREES, GET UP HIGH!"

The delegates scrambled. Jack hastily climbed up and held on tightly as he heaved Tom into the branches. The wolf bounded up the hill.

"What's going on?" Jack asked.

"Tsunami."

A few miles out to sea a surging wall of water gathered momentum.

Jack gripped the branch. "Bloody hell, Tom."

Tom looked along the trees. The horrified delegates huddled in twos and threes clinging to the branches and each other.

"HOLD ON AS TIGHT AS YOU CAN!"

Tom stared out at a mass of dark green that had grown as tall as a skyscraper. The tranquil ocean had transformed into a wall of terror. An ear-splitting roar charged towards them, and the sun disappeared as the water stretched up high before crashing down and sweeping the village aside like a paper cup.

Foaming rapids rushed by, rising higher and higher. Tom and Jack scrambled further up the tree.

The delegates struggled, but Tom couldn't help them. Some had already been dragged inland. Those still in the trees screamed for mercy. Jack tugged him.

"Tom, the tree's going."

Tom's foot slipped as the tree plunged into the foaming current. He gulped down muddy saltwater and fought to stay afloat. The rapids sucked them under. Grabbing splintered driftwood, he and Jack heaved themselves across it. The torrent rushed them further into the hills, bouncing them off craggy rocks and fallen trees. Four times Jack slipped from the raft and four times Tom dragged him back.

Further inland, the river lost momentum and gently deposited them on a grass bank where Tom lost consciousness.

169

He didn't know how long he'd been out for but he sensed a stillness. The wolf licked his ear and he opened his eyes wearily. He wanted to shut them again, to go to sleep and wake up in his bedroom. His foot throbbed and ached. Someone shook him.

"Tom?" Jack said. "Tom."

Tom rolled over and sighed. "You all right?"

He nodded. "Just some bruised ribs."

Tom studied him. Fresh tears had marked his muddy cheeks. He sat up.

"What's wrong? What's happened?"

"I went for a walk." He gestured toward the group. "Some of them came too."

"What? What did you see?"

"Things I don't ever wanna see again. I've seen dead bodies, not necessarily in one piece, complete devastation. It's the worst thing ever. It looks like a war zone. They all saw it, look at 'em."

Many delegates sat weeping, some too shaken to speak, others held their head in their hands. He put his hand on Jack's shoulder.

"Jack, remember, this is what might happen. This is how Mother Earth will react if we don't change. This might not happen."

The delegates looked up. Tom's head buzzed. He flinched as he put weight on his foot.

"Listen everyone. We've got the power and influence to change this. This is the path we're on now, but it doesn't have to be. There's always a choice, another path, but it's up to us. We're taking too much and we're not considering any other species on the planet, or earth itself for that matter."

The Prime Minister got to his feet.

"Tom, we'd like to go back." His colleagues nodded and murmured their agreement. "We'll do what we can to change.

We've already started in some areas. You must know about the changes we've already made."

"Me too," said another delegate as he got up; and then another, until two thirds stood. Those that couldn't stand held their hands high. The US President staggered forward.

"Tom, you've heard us. We'll go back and try to change. I can't take anymore of this. I've broken my arm and my head's split at the back here. These people need treatment."

Tom's head buzzed and he looked anxiously at the bruised and battered delegates in front of him.

"Telling the skulls you'll try isn't enough."

The news physically drained the delegates. With the eagle in flight and the wolf's senses aroused, a blazing bolt of lightening scorched the ground, temporarily blinding them. Tom grabbed Jack.

The brightness vanished and they hovered a few feet above a city street; a deserted city with empty shops and restaurants. Tom didn't like it. Cities need people.

Jack nudged him. "Look."

People appeared in front of them, emerging from nowhere. Just one or two at first, but then more. Tom studied them closely; it was like seeing a photograph being developed with more and more images taking their place and going about their business.

Tom chewed his lip. "What's going on?"

Jack flinched. "There's my parents. And Ed!"

Tom caught his breath. "There's your cousin. There's Mr Jenner, the farmer, and our school mates. There's Grandad. And look! There's Davvers and Chief Satowa."

Jack grabbed him. "There's your parents over there."

Tom looked around. All of the delegates pointed and shouted to their own friends and family, but their greetings went unseen and unheard. He sighed longingly. He'd give anything to go down and be with his family. He realised just how much they meant to him. Something above caught his eye.

"That's funny," he said to Jack.

"What?"

"That plane." His eyes opened wide in horror. "Oh no!"

"What?"

"They're the planes I saw. In my vision. It was 2012; they were gathering in a square, a massive army." He turned to Jack. "They were getting ready for war."

The black triangular plane flew towards them and ejected one solitary bomb. Tom shook uncontrollably. Their families! Their friends! Please stop it, don't let this happen.

The bomb exploded.

Tom fell to his knees as a sonic boom shattered his eardrums and swatted him like a fly. A blinding flash turned the sky white. The delegates shrieked as the fireball transformed into a colossal mushroom cloud.

Their loved ones below stood, defenceless, as clouds of searing ash rushed through them. Tom closed his eyes and waited for death. His skin blistered, the delegates wailed and screamed and the victims below turned to dust.

The nuclear wind continued its path of destruction, leaving nothing but death for as far as the eye could see.

Tom and the delegates floated down to a carpet of grey dust and gazed on a scene of utter desolation.

Day had turned to night. The bright blue summer had turned to an endless bleak winter. What buildings stood had become shells and human flesh had turned to oddly-shaped ash sculptures.

The numbed delegates wandered aimlessly, struggling to find survivors, but Tom knew it wouldn't happen. How could anyone survive this?

Jack sat and sobbed. Tom limped to where he thought his parents had been. Delegates wept over loved ones and begged for forgiveness. Tom wiped the tears from his eyes and searched for his family.

He found them, among those that had huddled together. Tom's mum and dad had been cuddling, sheltering each other. Salty tears poured silently as he touched the ash with his fingertips.

His head buzzed. He clenched his fists and punched the air.

"NO! NO MORE!" He dropped to his knees, screaming. "YOU'VE TAKEN EVERYTHING. THERE'S NO MORE TO TAKE."

The delegates looked on pitifully, each and every one of them bereft and beaten.

"Tom!" The Prime Minister trembled violently with shock. "We understand. We'll work together to protect this planet. None of us want this."

Tom closed his eyes. Only the skulls will know. They must decide.

The skulls launched them high into the skies. Tom's heart sunk and he prepared for the worst. The winds sucked them down in a spiral. The skies cleared, city lights clustered and blue seas rolled gently. The whirlwind pulled them further down through a warm channel of air.

They crashed through the gaping hole of the conference centre and Tom hurtled into the podium on the stage. Jack smashed into him. Dust and rubble returned to the ceiling as the damaged roof repaired itself.

Tom peered out of one eye. The auditorium resembled a battlefield. Paramedics and native elders rushed to help the delegates. They looked in a bad way. People made up home-made stretchers, applied dressings and made splints from broken chairs.

He closed his eyes. That's it, all done. The last thing he heard was Jack's voice.

"Davvers? I can't feel a pulse."
Then everything went black.

CHAPTER TWENTY-NINE

Two weeks later, Tom strolled along the Cornish shoreline; the wolf trotted happily beside him.

The town hadn't changed, but Tom remembered that only a month had passed since he'd found the skull. He threw a stick for the wolf and recalled Jack's memories about the moment he'd blacked out.

"I thought you were dead," he'd said, "but Davvers found a pulse. Then Chief Satowa came over and told some of his mates to take you outside. They put you in a truck and we all went off to a reservation."

Tom had vague memories of bumping about in a car.

"Then they prepared a sweat lodge. I weren't allowed in, but I heard the elders chanting and praying and stuff. Satowa stayed with you the whole time. You didn't wake up for three days."

Tom smiled at his first clear memory.

"You sleep well, my grandson," Chief Satowa had said.

Once properly awake, Satowa smiled warmly.

"My grandson, the keepers of the skulls, the ancients and those that live by their prophesy are pleased. The skulls, I think, took you on a most dangerous path. The visions I had during meditation were most disturbing."

"Is everyone all right?" Tom asked gingerly. "I mean, no one died or anything?"

Satowa shook his head. "The skulls would not allow it. Many broken bones, cuts, shock. Enough to make a difference."

"And have we? Made a difference?"

Chief Satowa nodded peacefully and got up.

"Many changes are being made. The men in power make it difficult to walk the same path. They are carving a new path. A path that will help all species and our Mother Earth. She will not be so angry at the end of the Fourth World."

"Is that still gonna happen!"

"Of course. But we create our own destiny. How we enter the Fifth World is our choice. But we have made a good start."

The wolf's bark brought Tom back from his thoughts. Davvers had opened up his cave. He jogged across and saw him packing up tea chests.

"What're you doing? You're not leaving?" Tom said.

Davvers stood up straight with a beaming smile. "Actually yes, but only up the road."

Tom frowned.

"I'm getting married."

"Married!"

"Yes. Once the skulls delivered their message, I suddenly wanted to get back to a house. I'm marrying the lady who bakes me cakes."

Tom nodded happily. "Shame about the cave – it's brilliant."

"Yours if you want it. Glad you're here, I wanted to ask you something."

He looked a little embarrassed. Tom had never seen him lost for words before.

"Tom, I'd be really honoured if you'd be my best man."

Tom's eyes opened wide. "Me!"

"Of course. I'd be proud to have you alongside on my big day."

Tom's face flushed. "I just did what I was told."

Davvers laughed. "Don't underestimate yourself. The skulls may be the orchestra, Tom, but you were the conductor." He fondled the wolf. "He staying with you?"

"Yes, he didn't wanna leave. The eagle stayed with Chief Satowa."

"Good show." He shot Tom an urgent look. "Aren't you supposed to be at school?"

Tom smiled. "Summer holidays. I'm back next week and I'm going to every class. Mr Griffith's even asked me to give a talk. We're pretty good friends now."

He sat down in one of the wing-back chairs.

"And Mum and Dad seem different. Well, actually, I think it's me that's different. Satowa helped me take a good look at myself."

Davvers carried on packing. "You should be different after the journey you've had. You can't come back the same person. Satowa's a wise man, he'll carry on teaching you, you know. You'll keep in touch with him?"

"Yes. He's taught me how to meet up with him in visions. Said something weird about going back with him to the buffalo time. Told me that to know our future, we must look to the past."

Davvers glanced up and grinned. "Your next adventure, perhaps."

Jack popped his head in. "Anyone home?"

Davvers rubbed his hands together and pulled the other chair across.

"Here we are again, the three of us together, just as we started out." He rummaged around in one of the tea chests and produced a gas stove and kettle. "How about some tea and cake before we move on with our lives?"

He grinned at Tom as they made themselves comfortable.

"That'll be great," Tom said.

He wondered if Satowa really meant what he'd said. He smiled to himself. School would be enough excitement for now.

The End

SOME FASCINATING TRIVIA
FOR THE READER

THE CRYSTAL SKULLS

The crystal skulls do exist! Go to any search engine on the Internet and type in 'crystal skulls' and find out about these extraordinary objects. The skulls are either in museums or private collections. Some are still lost, although it's said that the Hopi tribe do know where the missing skulls are, but will not reveal this to anyone.

The legend speaks of thirteen skulls, all able to talk and sing. They are said to hold knowledge of the history of the world and the evolution of mankind. The legend states that the skulls will come together to reveal important information that is vital to the survival of the human race.

Scientific tests on the skulls reveal that it should have been impossible for people in the ancient world to carve them. Without modern tools it is estimated that it would have taken three hundred years to carve just one crystal skull. Those tests also suggest that the skulls would have been capable of storing information.

*

THE MAYAN CALENDAR

Information about the Mayan calendar, again, can be found via any search engine on the Internet. The Maya are said to have charted time accurately over a span of more than ten million years, including all astronomical events. The world of the fifth sun begins, according to Mayan legend, on 21st December 2012. Many see this as the 'end of the world'. However, the Mayans and most Native American tribes see this period as a time of rebirth; a new era where people will live in both peace and harmony with Mother Earth.

*

CHIEF SEATTLE'S SPEECH

At the end of chapter 11, Tom holds a scrappy piece of paper with a small statement on it. This is an adaptation of part of a long speech made by an insightful Native American called Chief Seattle.

Chief Seattle lived in the mid-1800s and became involved, as did many tribal chiefs, in the struggle against the new settlers who took over their lands and killed millions of their people. No one is completely sure about the exact words spoken by Chief Seattle and the speech he made to the men in power. There are many versions in print but all say pretty much the same thing – that mankind is in no position to buy or take anything from Mother Earth or the Great Spirit. Without Mother Earth, we would not be here.

THE BREATH OF MOTHER EARTH

Yes, the earth does breathe; there are many places across the globe where you can do the same as Tom, and stick your head into a blowhole to feel the breath of Mother Earth. My own experience was at a national park, called Wupatki, just north of Flagstaff in Arizona.

Scientists tell us that the air in these holes either blows out or breathes in, depending on the air pressure above ground.

So, although it's scientifically proven that this is down to weather, I prefer the Native American belief about the earth breathing.

*

THE PIRI REIS MAP
In chapter 20, Davvers refers to a map and I've based this, very loosely, on the Piri Reis map. The Piri Reis map was found in the 15th century and is said to be a copy of a much older document. This map accurately charts the land under the ice (one mile thick) at Antarctica. Again, type 'Piri Reis' into any search engine and you can find out lots about this ancient document. Here's some amazing facts for you to ponder:

- Many scientists believe that the last time the Antarctic was ice-free was between 13000 and 9000 BC. According to our traditional history books, the first civilisation came into being around 3000 BC, so who had the technology to map the land beneath the ice before this date?
- The Piri Reis map is drawn assuming the earth is round. (The earliest people to discover the spherical earth were the ancient Greeks, 2500 years ago. Who could have known this thousands of years before?)
- In 1953, a chief engineer with the US Navy stated that the only way to draw a map with such accuracy was by using aerial surveying. Who, 6000 years ago, had aeroplanes?

*

THE LOST CITY OF ATLANTIS

The explanation about Atlantis, given in chapter 20, is probably the most well known. There are so many stories about Atlantis and where the lost city may be situated, that it would be impossible for me to speculate. As with the other subjects here, simply type 'Atlantis' into a search engine and you can make your own mind up.